A Note from Theo

Scoring goals is great, but you get just as much satisfaction from setting them up. Football is a team game and no one can score goals without the help of their team-mates, as Tulsi learns in this story.

So keep on practising – and make sure you play as part of a team as you will all enjoy it more together.

Theo Walcott

Access your secret bonus content!

Every Theo Walcott T.J. book has SECRET bonus

content online! It could be a cool download,

football tips, a secret story . . . or something

even more exciting!

Check it out at:

www.theowalcottbooks.co.uk/winninggoal

Also available by Theo Walcott:

T.J. AND THE HAT-TRICK

T.J. AND THE PENALTY

T.J. AND THE CUP RUN

THEO WALCOTT

WITH PAUL MAY

T.J. AND THE
WINNING GOAL

ILLUSTRATIONS BY JERRY PARIS

CORGI BOOKS

T.J. AND THE WINNING GOAL
A CORGI BOOK 978 0 552 56248 5

Published in Great Britain by Corgi Books,
an imprint of Random House Children's Publishers UK
A Random House Group Company

This edition published 2010

5 7 9 10 8 6

Set in 14/22pt Meta Normal

Corgi Books are published by Random House Children's Publishers UK
61–63 Uxbridge Road, London W5 5SA

www.**randomhousechildrens**.co.uk
www.randomhouse.co.uk

Addresses for companies within The Random House Group Limited can be found at:
www.randomhouse.co.uk/offices.htm

THE RANDOM HOUSE GROUP Limited Reg. No. 954009

A CIP catalogue record for this book is available from the British Library.

Printed and bound in Great Britain by Clays Ltd, St Ives PLC

SQUAD SHEET

TJ: A skilful forward with an outstanding turn of speed. He has an incredibly powerful shot, and he's good in the air too.

Tulsi: A strong, powerful striker. When she has the ball at her feet all she thinks about is scoring!

Rodrigo: He's from Portugal and he doesn't speak much English, but he's a wizard with a football in midfield or defence.

Rafi: A midfielder who never stops running and tackling. His mazy runs are legendary and he always brings a ball to school!

Leila: An excellent tackler and a natural holding midfielder.

Tommy: When he's not skateboarding he's a fearsome tackler in Parkview's defence.

Jamie: Big, strong, fit – and the team's keeper. He'll stop anything heading towards him!

Danny: He's not popular, but he's a terrific defender and Parkview can't do without him.

Ariyan: He can play anywhere and do a good job for the team. A really useful squad member.

Rob: He can read the game and set up clever moves from the midfield. But can he control his nerves when he's out on the pitch?

Ebony: She has pace and a killer instinct for scoring goals. She's fighting hard for a first-team place as a striker.

FOR SEBASTIAN AND AURORA

CHAPTER 1

'You came!' said Tulsi. 'That's great! Now you'll really see something.'

'Like what?' asked TJ, smiling.

'Like me scoring goals,' replied Tulsi. 'That's what I do. I'm off to get changed. I'll see you in a bit.'

Tulsi Patel was the striker in Parkview School's football team. But long before Parkview School even *had* a team, Tulsi had been playing for Canby Road Girls in the Sunday League. She'd been trying to get her friends from Parkview to come and watch her play on a Sunday morning for ages.

Now, at last, they were here.

TJ was a speedy forward with a lethal shot who had only arrived at Parkview School at the beginning of the year. His friend Jamie, the spiky-haired, cheerful giant standing beside him, was the team's goalkeeper. Scouts from Wanderers, the nearby Premier League club, had spotted TJ and Jamie playing for the school team, and now they both attended a Player Development Centre in the local Sports Centre every week. Their friends, Rafi and Rob, had come with them today. They all watched as Tulsi walked off to the dressing rooms in a low brick clubhouse at the side of the playing field.

'What do you think?' asked Jamie. 'Will she play the same way she always does?'

'Are you kidding?' laughed Rafi, bouncing the football that he carried everywhere. 'Tulsi's always been the same, and I've been playing football with her since she was four years old.'

'He's right,' agreed Rob. 'I remember her when we were in the Reception class. She used to stand by the goal and scream at everyone to give her the ball.'

'And I suppose you wrote that down,' Jamie said, laughing.

'No,' replied Rob, who loved filling notebooks with statistics. 'But I did a picture. I brought it with me. I knew you'd want to see.'

He pulled a notebook from his pocket. On the cover it said: TULSI MATCH STATS.

'Hey,' said Rafi. 'Have you got one of those for all of us?'

Rob nodded sheepishly. 'Information is important,' he told them. 'After all, one day someone might want to write the history of Parkview football team. Look, here's Tulsi.'

He opened the notebook to reveal a crumpled, yellowing drawing of a face with

3

wild, staring eyes and a mass of brown hair.
Rob's friends laughed. 'That's *exactly* what
she used to be like,' said Jamie.

'Why is her face blue?' asked TJ.

'I was only four,' replied Rob with a grin.

'What are you all looking at?' demanded
Tulsi, running up to them in her training top
and tracksuit bottoms.

'Nothing,' said Rob, snapping the notebook shut.

'Hey, wait a minute. That's my name on
there. Let me see!'

She grabbed the book from Rob and
opened it. 'That's you,' said Jamie, as Tulsi

stared at the screaming, blue-faced child. 'You haven't changed much, have you?'

'Ha ha,' said Tulsi, shoving Jamie away. 'You should have been looking at my stats. Look at all these goals I've scored. You'd better get ready to add some more, Rob. We're on that pitch over there. Kick off in ten minutes. We're playing Norton Girls. If we beat them we'll go top of the league.'

Tulsi ran off. The Canby Road playing field was on the edge of town. It was huge, and there seemed to be hundreds of people playing football, from the tiniest little kids on small pitches near the dressing rooms to full-scale grown-up matches on the pitches far away, near where the trees and fields of the countryside began.

'Over there,' said TJ, pointing, and they headed for the pitch where the two teams of girls were warming up. Both teams had brought plenty of supporters and they were grouped behind the tape on one side of the pitch. 'There's Tulsi's mum,' said Jamie. 'Hello, Mrs Patel.'

'Nice to see you boys,' said Mrs Patel. 'Would you like to share my umbrella?'

TJ realized that a drizzly rain had started to fall. 'It's OK, Mrs Patel,' said Rob. 'I've brought one.' He unfurled an enormous multi-coloured golf umbrella. 'Well?' he said, when he saw his friends staring at him. 'I don't want my notebook to get wet, do I?'

'Very sensible,' laughed Mrs Patel. 'Let's hope it's an exciting match. I think they're about to start. COME ON, CANBY ROAD!' she yelled, in an enormous voice that made them all jump. Tulsi looked over at them and grinned, as Norton kicked off.

'Not bad,' commented Rob after a few minutes. Canby Road were working hard and passing the ball well, but neither team had managed a shot on goal yet. 'The girl with the curly red hair is good,' Rob added appreciatively. 'She must be Kira Jones, the captain. Tulsi told me about her. She hasn't lost the ball once so far. Look at that!'

The red-haired girl was running Canby Road's midfield, and now she turned cleverly away from the player who was marking her. Suddenly she had some space, and she had her head up, looking for a pass. Tulsi yelled for the ball. 'Don't do it,' muttered Rob to himself. 'There are too many defenders.'

TJ glanced at Rob, then back at the pitch. The midfielder had reached the same conclusion as Rob, and played the ball out to the wing. The Canby Road attack finally fizzled out. Then TJ and Rob saw Tulsi complaining to Kira Jones, who turned away.

'I don't know why she won't pass to Tulsi,' said Mrs Patel, when a few more minutes had passed and the end of the first half was approaching. 'They used to pass to her all the time.'

'It's because she's always marked very tightly,' Rob said. 'Tulsi's been playing in this league for two years now. All the teams know what she does and they've worked out how to stop her. Look!'

A Canby Road player had finally played the ball to Tulsi, who was standing close to the edge of the Norton penalty area, just as she always did. She controlled the ball and turned to run past the defender who was marking her. 'Go on, Tulsi!' yelled TJ. The others were shouting too, and Tulsi's mum was shouting louder than any of them. Tulsi beat the defender and pulled back her foot to shoot. But a second defender was there, blocking the shot and bringing the ball away to start another Norton attack.

The Canby Road supporters groaned.

When the whistle blew for half time, neither team had scored, and Tulsi walked off the pitch shaking her head in disgust.

CHAPTER 2

'What are you doing?' TJ asked Rob, who was
scribbling busily in his notebook.

'I'm just mapping out Tulsi's runs,'
replied Rob. 'It's not as hard as you'd think,
because most of the time she just waits on
the edge of the area. Look.'

Rob's diagram was like a small, spiky ball.
There were one or two little spikes where
she'd run to either corner of the area, or
back a little way towards the centre circle. TJ
laughed. 'It's like the one you did the first
time we played a match,' he said.

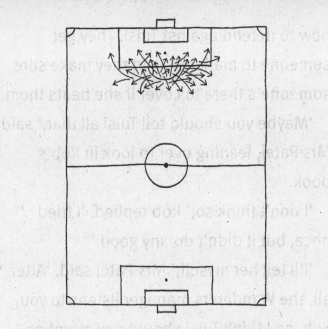

'You're right,' said Rob. 'And in every other match.'

He flipped through the pages and TJ saw that all the diagrams were the same. 'But Tulsi's a really good player,' said TJ. 'And she scores goals.'

'Not as many as last season,' Rob told him, shaking his head. 'Last season she got fifteen. She was top scorer in this league. But she's only scored four so far this season. The other teams have worked out how to defend against Tulsi. They get someone to mark her, and they make sure someone's there to cover if she beats them.'

'Maybe you should tell Tulsi all that,' said Mrs Patel, leaning over to look in Rob's book.

'I don't think so,' Rob replied. 'I tried once, but it didn't do any good.'

'I'll tell her myself,' Mrs Patel said. 'After all, the Wanderers manager listens to you, Rob, so I think Tulsi should pay attention.'

Rob was embarrassed. It was true that the Wanderers manager had taken his advice once, but he hated people talking about it. 'No, please, Mrs Patel. It won't do any good. Honestly.'

Mrs Patel shook her head. Then she smiled. 'Maybe she'll score this half,' she said. 'That's what we need.'

Not long after the kick off, Tulsi's chance arrived. Two of the Norton players collided with each other in the centre circle and the ball ran free to Kira Jones. She sprinted forward. In front of her, Tulsi had her back to goal with a defender right behind her as usual. The midfielder hit a sharp pass to Tulsi's feet and carried on running into the penalty area, screaming for a return pass.

Tulsi ignored her. She back-heeled the ball, deceiving her marker, and turned to take a left-foot shot. But once again a second defender was waiting. She blocked Tulsi's shot and played a swift pass into midfield. The Norton players streamed forward and scored a perfect breakaway goal.

'Bad luck, Tulsi,' called Mrs Patel. 'Better luck next time! Come on, Canby!'

Rob just shook his head. 'That was a brilliant run that Kira Jones made,' he said. 'She was taking advantage of how they put that extra defender on Tulsi. Tulsi should have passed. If she had then it would be one–nil to Canby.'

'I think Kira Jones agrees with you,' said Jamie. 'Look at her face!'

The Canby Road captain was walking back into her own half. She didn't even glance at Tulsi. And before Canby Road could kick off again, TJ saw their coach waving from the touchline.

'Oh no,' said Rob. 'She's taking Tulsi off.'

Tulsi glanced towards the touchline, and quickly looked away again. Then the coach called her name, and she couldn't pretend any longer. She walked very slowly off the pitch, her head down. A small girl with a blonde pony tail ran on to replace her. They saw Tulsi speak angrily to the coach and then walk off towards the changing rooms. 'I'd better go and make sure she's all right,' said Mrs Patel anxiously. 'Thank you for coming, boys.'

'This is horrible,' said Jamie. 'I wish

we weren't here.'

'I think it's going to get worse,' Rob said. 'This new girl is pretty good.'

The blonde girl was a very different player from Tulsi. From the moment she arrived on the pitch she began to make energetic darting runs – into the corners, back towards the centre circle, and from side to side along the line of defenders. Kira Jones won the ball in midfield and instantly hit a pass towards the corner flag. The new girl was after it in a flash. She caught up with the ball and laid it back to Kira, then sprinted towards the goal. Kira played the ball into her path, but instead of shooting she pulled it back unselfishly across the goal and one of her team-mates smashed it into the net.

'That was a proper team goal,' said Rob, making a note of all the passes. 'It's almost as if Canby have an extra player now.'

'Here they come again,' said Rafi, who had stopped messing around with his ball and was watching the game intently. 'This is pretty good.'

Canby Road tore the Norton team to pieces. They scored three quick goals and ran out 4–1 winners. 'How is Tulsi going to get back in the team?' said TJ. 'They were a lot better *without* her.'

'It's not that simple,' said Rob. 'Tulsi's right about one thing. She's very good at scoring goals. That other girl didn't score once. Tulsi could easily be as good as her. Better. She just has to listen to what Mr Wood says. It's not as if he hasn't told her. It's not as if *we* haven't told her.'

They walked back towards the changing rooms and saw Mrs Patel emerging with Tulsi beside her. They walked to the car and Tulsi didn't look back.

'Hey, Tulsi,' TJ called after her. 'Tough luck.

I bet the next time you'll get a hat-trick.'

The car doors slammed. TJ looked helplessly at his friends. They'd all seen the tears on Tulsi's face. They waved half-heartedly as the Patels' car drew away.

CHAPTER 3

On Monday morning Tulsi was still in a terrible mood. 'She shouldn't have taken me off,' she said. 'If they passed to me more then I'd score more goals. It's obvious.'

'Right,' said TJ. 'It was a shame. Still, at least your team won. You're top of the league.'

'I suppose. But now Carla Stamp has got my place. Everyone says she played really well.'

'That's true,' agreed Rob, and Tulsi's face fell. 'But she didn't score any goals,' Rob continued. 'And that's what you're good at.'

'Hey, thanks, Rob,' said Tulsi, brightening up a little.

'You lot,' Jamie interrupted. 'The bell's gone. We don't want to annoy Mr Wood. He'll be picking the team soon for the Regional Tournament.'

Parkview School had recently won their District Tournament, and that meant they would soon be travelling to play against the best teams from all over their part of England. None of them wanted to miss out on that. So they ran to class.

'Settle down, everyone,' Mr Wood said as his pupils filed in. 'We have two special visitors today. You'll probably remember them.'

Mr Wood always dressed smartly in the classroom, but today he was wearing a dark-grey suit that looked new and a white shirt that seemed to shine with a light of its own. Then TJ saw the visitors and his heart sank.

The inspectors were back, Mr Turvey and Mr Grayson. He couldn't see why Mr Wood should be pleased. The last time the inspectors had been here they had made all the teachers miserable, especially Mr Burrows, the head. But then TJ realized that the inspectors were smiling – even Mr Grayson, who TJ had never seen smile before.

'We've come to give you good news,' Mr Turvey said. 'It's been absolutely remarkable the way this school has improved in such a short time, and we've written a report that says so. I don't know how you've managed to get all this painting and decorating done—'

'It was our mums and dads,' Jamie interrupted, putting his hand up.

'And grandmas and grandpas,' added Rafi.

'Everyone helped,' said TJ.

'Indeed,' said Mr Grayson. 'Everything has changed. We've seen the tremendous project work on food and football – and the school's outstanding achievements in sport. I believe you have four football teams now, Mr Wood?'

Mr Wood smiled. 'That was Mr Burrows' idea,' he told them. 'The school has gone a little crazy about football.'

'Well,' said Mr Turvey, 'you are all about to win an award for being the region's most improved school. You deserve it. And jolly good luck in the regional football tournament too.'

'Hmmm,' said Mr Wood when the inspectors had left. 'Don't let all that praise go to your heads. We're going to need more than luck to win the tournament. You remember how hard the last one was. We have to be really fit. So this afternoon in Games we're going to do the beep test again. We'll see if your fitness has improved since the last time.'

TJ glanced round at Tulsi. She had a big smile on her face. The last time they'd done a beep test, on a school visit to the Wanderers training ground, Tulsi had been the fittest person in the whole of Year Six.

'Do you think you're going to win again?' asked TJ at lunch time.

'Sure,' said Tulsi. 'I'm just as fit as I was then.'

'Well, I'm going to try and beat you,' laughed TJ. 'All the extra training I've been doing must have helped a bit.'

Outside on the playground that afternoon Mr Wood laid out rows of cones, then he sent Year Six off to jog around the field to warm up. 'Line up here,' he said when they returned.

TJ looked along the line and saw that

nobody was breathing hard. They were all definitely fitter than before. 'When you hear a beep, run to the next set of cones,' Mr Wood said. 'At the next beep you turn and run back. The beeps will speed up, and once you've been late for two beeps I'll call you out. Everyone ready? Off you go.'

Rob was running alongside TJ.

'Definitely better,' he said after the first few runs, glancing at his watch. 'Last time, the first person dropped out after two minutes. We've been going for four already.'

Just as Rob spoke TJ heard Mr Wood's whistle and the first person jogged over to wait beside him. Slowly at first, other people dropped behind the beats until only about half the class were left. TJ looked along the line again. 'Jamie's still going,' TJ said to Rob. Jamie had been one of the first to go before.

'What do you expect?' said Rob, smiling,

as they turned to the beep. 'After all that trouble we went to, to help him get fit.'

The next beep caught TJ by surprise. He was late. 'Get a move on,' said Rob, gritting his teeth. 'This is where it starts to hurt.'

'Come on, Tulsi,' called Mr Wood. 'You can do it!'

The group waiting beside Mr Wood had grown. Everyone who was still running had played in the school team at some time. Beside Rob and TJ there were Rafi and Portuguese Rodrigo, and Tommy the skate-boarder. They were urging each other on in a group. Then came Jamie, Ariyan, Leila, Ebony, Cameron, Danny and Tulsi.

But Tulsi was falling behind. TJ couldn't believe it, but he had no breath to say anything more to Rob. At the next beep they heard the whistle, and Tulsi was walking back to Mr Wood.

The beeps came faster and faster. Now

there were only four runners left: TJ, Jamie, Rob and Rodrigo. At the next beep Rodrigo and Jamie were finished, but TJ hardly noticed. All he could think of were those terrible beeps. He saw Rob pull half a metre ahead of him, and sure enough at the next turn Rob was on time and TJ was half a second late. TJ put on a spurt and caught up with Rob, but his lungs were bursting and his muscles felt as if they were on fire. Another beep, and another, and suddenly TJ knew he was beaten. His legs simply wouldn't do what he told them any more. He struggled to the side and bent over, gasping for air, as the whole class applauded Rob,

turning, running, turning, and finally stopping.

'Absolutely fantastic,' said Mr Wood. 'I haven't checked the scores properly yet, but I'm pretty sure that every single one of you has improved.'

'I haven't,' muttered Tulsi.

'But you have,' Mr Wood told her. 'It's just that everyone else has too. Now let's get the footballs out and practise some skills.'

CHAPTER 4

'Cheer up,' Jamie said to Tulsi, as they walked over to the playing field. 'It's not as bad as it seems. You heard what Mr Wood said. We're *all* much fitter. And we'll need to be for the tournament.'

'But I *liked* being the fittest person in the school,' replied Tulsi. 'I thought I still was.'

'Come on,' said Jamie. 'We can be partners. You're definitely better at ball control than me. You can help me.'

'It's a good thing we've got Jamie,' TJ said to Rob, as they picked up a ball and went to work in one of the ten-metre squares marked out on the field. 'If anyone can make Tulsi feel better it's him.'

Rob nodded in agreement. 'We'd better start,' he said. 'What did Mr Wood tell us to do?'

'Left foot then right foot,' TJ replied. 'Pass and control. Then pass, control and move.'

They had only been working for a couple of minutes when Rob stopped. He put his foot on the ball and pointed at the playground. 'Who's that?' he asked.

TJ looked where Rob was pointing. The head teacher, Mr Burrows, was walking towards them with a young man and a taller bald one who had an enormous camera slung around his neck. Mr Wood stopped the session and called everyone together.

'As you know,' Mr Burrows said, 'the inspectors have produced a truly excellent report on our school. When I told our local paper about it they were very keen to do a feature on us. And about all of you. This is Mr, er . . .'

'Call me Dan,' said the young man, whipping a notebook from his pocket.

'Just like yours,' TJ whispered to Rob.

'You can keep on with what you were doing,' Dan said. 'Barry here'll come round and take some snaps.'

'Off you go, everyone,' Mr Burrows urged them. 'Our training is second to none,' TJ heard him saying to the reporter. 'Our Mr Wood is a magnificent coach . . .'

TJ and Rob went back to work. They carried on as if it was just a normal Games lesson, though it wasn't easy to concentrate, as the photographer circled around them and the flash from the camera dazzled them. 'That'll do,' Mr Wood said finally. 'You've worked hard this afternoon. Let's have some fun to finish off. Five-a-side. I'll pick the teams.'

TJ found himself in a team with Rafi, Tommy, Cameron and Leila. 'I'll go in goal,' Leila volunteered. 'I'd like to try. I've never done it before.'

'We'll swap if you let one in,' TJ said, as they put on green training bibs. The other team were in red, and they had Jamie in goal, Tulsi up front and Rob in midfield.

'This is going to be tough,' Rafi said.

'Not if you mark Tulsi properly,' TJ replied. 'Rob told me what to do, so it'll serve him right if they lose. Cameron, you mark her. Tommy, you just have to be ready if she goes past Cameron. You don't need to worry about whoever you were marking, because when Tulsi's in on goal she only thinks about one thing – scoring.'

The others nodded. 'It might just work,' Cameron said.

The Greens kicked off with TJ playing on his own up front. He gave the ball to Rafi who set off on a mazy dribble and then back-heeled it to Leila. Leila played the ball quickly to TJ's feet and he slipped past Rob with a lightning burst of speed. *Rob might be able to keep going longer,* thought TJ, *but I bet I'll always beat him over twenty metres.*

He considered shooting, but then he looked up and saw Jamie. He was perfectly positioned in front of his goal, so TJ pulled the ball back for Rafi who was racing towards the penalty area at top speed. It would have been perfect if Rafi hadn't tripped over the ball. He tumbled head over heels two or three times and the ball trickled harmlessly forward to a very relieved Jamie, who grinned. 'Close!' he said, laughing, as Rafi jumped to his feet. 'You're supposed to kick it, not fall over it!'

Before Rafi could think of a clever reply, Jamie had rolled the ball to Ariyan and Rafi had to chase back hard. But he couldn't catch Ariyan in time and Ariyan gave the ball to Rob who instantly snapped a pass to Tulsi. She turned and came face to face with Cameron. Cameron hesitated as Tulsi took the ball towards him, and Tulsi took her chance, jumping neatly over his out-stretched foot.

'Yes!' cried Rob, sprinting into space down the right wing. But Tulsi ignored him. She could see the goal and she was going to shoot. She was a striker, after all! She took one final touch – and Tommy whipped the ball away from her. She was already committed to the shot, but her foot connected with empty air and she landed flat on her back with a thump that knocked all the breath out of her – just as the camera flashed.

When the game finished, the photographer was waiting at the edge of the pitch. 'I'll need some names,' he said. 'We have to make sure everyone knows who you are. Your teachers will check with your mums and dads if it's OK for you to have your pictures in the paper.'

'Please,' said Tulsi. 'You won't use that picture you took of me, will you? When I fell over.'

'Of course not, love,' replied the photographer. 'I thought you were going to score a brilliant goal. There's bound to be a better one than that. Now, tell me how to spell your name . . .'

CHAPTER 5

Later that week Mr Wood announced the squad for a friendly match against their old rivals, Hillside School. 'At least I'm in the team,' Tulsi said gloomily. 'I was beginning to think I wouldn't be.'

'Don't worry so much,' Jamie told her. 'You know you're our star striker.'

'Well, I don't feel like one,' Tulsi replied.

The friendly match was being played on Friday afternoon at Parkview. Mr Coggins, the caretaker, was hard at work all Friday morning preparing the pitch and marking out the white lines. At lunch time TJ was surprised to see Mr Wood walk out onto the playground. TJ and his friends were kicking Rafi's ball around as usual.

'Tulsi,' Mr Wood said. 'Have you got a few minutes?'

'OK,' she said. 'What's it about?'

But Mr Wood didn't reply, and when Tulsi returned she didn't want to talk.

'What did he want?' asked Jamie.

'Nothing.'

'Come on, Tulsi,' Rafi said. 'He wouldn't have called you inside for nothing, would he?'

'Let's have a penalty competition,' Tulsi said, grabbing the ball from Rafi. 'I feel like kicking something really hard. Who's going in goal?'

'Not me,' said Rafi. 'Not if you're in that kind of mood.'

'I'm not scared,' laughed Jamie. 'It'll be good practice for this afternoon.'

He stood in front of the goalposts painted on the wall and saved every one of Tulsi's first four shots. Each shot was harder than the one before, and with every save Tulsi's face darkened. She ran up and hit her fifth penalty and the ball flew up and over the wall into the garden beyond. They all stared after it. There was a thud as the ball hit a wall, and then a loud clattering and the outraged miaow of a cat.

Tulsi put her hands to her head. They waited for angry shouts from the garden, but none came. 'It'll be OK,' Jamie said. 'They must be out. They'll just chuck it back later.'

'Don't be stupid,' Tulsi said. 'You heard the noise. I bet something's broken and now I'm going to be in trouble. You know I am.'

Tulsi walked away. 'What's up with her?' said Rafi. 'It's my ball she's lost. I'm the one who should be complaining.'

'Tulsi's fed up, that's all,' said TJ. 'I don't

know what Mr Wood said to her, but it definitely put her in a bad mood.'

At two o'clock TJ looked out of the classroom window and saw the Hillside minibus arriving. Since Mr Wood had started the school team at the beginning of the year they had played against Hillside more than any other team, and because Hillside was the nearest school to Parkview they often met the kids from Hillside for kickarounds in the park. One of their players, Deng, went to the same Player Development Centre as TJ and Jamie. It was funny, thought TJ, but the Hillside players almost felt like friends now. At least until the match began.

As they got changed TJ couldn't help thinking that it was a shame Danny wasn't in the squad. He hadn't been coming to training lately, so it wasn't surprising that Mr Wood hadn't picked him. Tommy and

Rodrigo were both excellent defenders, especially when they had won the ball and were attacking, but if you needed someone to mark an opposition player out of the game then Danny was the best. If they were going to do well in the Regional Tournament they were going to need all their best players.

'Come on, TJ,' called Jamie from the door. TJ looked up and realized that everyone had gone. 'What were you doing?' asked Jamie, as they walked outside.

'Thinking,' said TJ. 'About Danny. I know you don't like him much, but I still think he's our best defender. I don't know why he stopped coming to training.'

'There's no point worrying about that now,' Jamie told him, breaking into a run. 'Come on, Mr Wood's waiting.'

As they warmed up TJ checked out the Hillside team and was relieved to see that none of their players were new. He remembered how Deng had arrived at Hillside in the middle of the previous term, turning Hillside from a good side into a formidable one with his lightning speed and wonderful touch. But then Parkview had discovered their own midfield genius in Rob, and that had made all the difference in the Cup Final. He was sure they could beat Hillside today, but they'd need to be at their best.

'OK,' said Mr Wood. 'We'll start with Tommy and Rodrigo in defence. Then Rafi and Rob in midfield and TJ and Tulsi up front. Jamie in goal. You all know your jobs so show me what you can do. Oh, and by the way, Rob, I've found someone to keep track of the match stats for you. Here he comes now.'

They all looked round and there was Mr Coggins. 'Mr Wood's given me a list,' he told them. 'I'll record goal attempts, passes, assists, corners, goal kicks . . .'

'It's OK, Mr C,' Mr Wood told him. 'We get the picture.'

'Mr Coggins,' said Rob. 'What's that you're wearing?'

'This?' said Mr Coggins. 'It's my old team blazer, that's what this is.'

The blazer had a big gold badge on the breast pocket. 'I was a good footballer when I was young,' Mr Coggins said. 'One of these days I'm going to tell you all about it. I—'

'Not right now, though,' Mr Wood interrupted with a smile. 'I think Mrs Singh is waiting to kick off. Tulsi, you can be captain today. And remember what we talked about. I know you can do it.'

CHAPTER 6

As soon as the match started TJ knew that
this was the best Parkview had ever played.
When Krissy Barton, the Hillside captain,
passed the ball back to Deng in midfield Rafi
was onto him at once, giving Deng no time
at all, and when Deng turned away from Rafi,
Rob was waiting. He stole the ball from
Deng's feet and before anyone could
challenge him he'd played it all the way
across the field to Tommy, who was moving
forward on the right wing.

Tommy clipped a pass back to Rafi, who
slid the ball over to Rodrigo, who hit it first

time to TJ. The Hillside players chased and harried, but hard as they tried, they couldn't even touch the ball. Mr Coggins noted down every pass in his notebook and the little kids from Reception who had come out to watch the game started counting out loud with a bit of help from their teacher.

The ball was back with Rob. He looked up and saw Tulsi making a diagonal run towards the far corner flag. Billy Martin, Hillside's tall blond defender, ran with her. TJ saw the space opening up in the centre of the pitch where Tulsi usually waited, and he took off at top speed. Rob saw his run and slotted the ball neatly through the crowded centre of the pitch into TJ's path. TJ didn't need to take a touch. As the goalkeeper raced out towards him he side-footed the ball past him into the net.

TJ flung his arms in the air, then ran to congratulate Rob on the pass. The Reception children on the touchline were shouting and cheering and running round in circles. 'We need to watch out,' Rob said, grinning. 'There might be a pitch invasion.'

'Nice run, Tulsi,' TJ said, as they waited for Hillside to restart the game. 'You've never done that before.'

'I thought Rob would play the ball into the corner,' Tulsi said.

'Yeah, and that's what their defenders thought too,' replied TJ. 'We wouldn't have scored if you hadn't done that.'

'*You* wouldn't have scored, that's what you mean,' said Tulsi. 'If Rob had passed to me then I might have scored.'

TJ shook his head. There was no doubt about it, Tulsi was really very fed up.

From their kick off Hillside now mounted their first attack of the game. Deng burst forward, swerving and side-stepping his way past both Rafi and Rob. Deng was an exceptionally talented footballer and TJ and Jamie both thought he would be the first of their friends at the Player Development Centre to be offered a trial at the Wanderers Academy. And he was unselfish too. He could easily have taken a shot himself, but having taken the Parkview midfield out of the game he now laid on a perfectly weighted pass for Krissy to smash the ball at Jamie's goal.

Jamie leaped and twisted in the air like a cat, and flung out an arm to punch the ball away. The punch was so strong that the ball rebounded all the way out to TJ, who had been running back to try and help out in the defence. He controlled it and played it infield to Rob, who had seen the chance of a quick counter-attack and was moving rapidly forward. TJ sprinted down the wing, and he saw to his surprise that Tulsi had made yet another run, this time back

44

towards the centre circle and once again the defender had gone with her. Her runs were pulling the Hillside defence all over the place, creating space for her team-mates. TJ moved in from the wing, calling for the ball, and Rob responded with another beautiful pass.

The counter-attack had happened so fast that the Hillside goalkeeper was still on the edge of his penalty area, as TJ received the ball from Rob. Tulsi had turned her defender again and was now racing towards the area herself, but the opportunity was too good to miss. TJ chipped the ball, not into Tulsi's path, but way over her head, and over the head of the defender, and over the wildly waving outstretched arms of the back-pedalling goalkeeper.

Goal!

TJ had chipped the keeper and scored! It was something he'd always wanted to do,

and now he'd done it. He punched the air
and ran round and round in circles until Rafi
grabbed him. 'Great goal, TJ!' laughed Rafi.

On the touchline even Mr Wood was
applauding. 'Great running, Tulsi,' he called.
'Good work, everyone. Keep it up.'

It was 2–0 to Parkview, but Tulsi wasn't
happy. 'I would have scored that time too,'
she said to TJ. 'You know what? If no one's
going to pass to me, then I'm not going to do
all that running around. It was Mr Wood's

idea but he was wrong. It's a waste of time.'

'No, it's not,' said Rob. 'It gives us more options, that's all.'

'I'll tell you what I'm going to do,' Tulsi said crossly. 'I'm going back where you can always find me. Near their goal. You pass to me and I score. How about that?'

Tulsi was as good as her word. As soon as Hillside kicked off again she trotted forward to the edge of the penalty area and waited. For the rest of the first half she hardly moved from her position while the rest of the team continued to pass the ball confidently. But now it was far more difficult for Rob to find telling passes. Whenever he played the ball forward to Tulsi, Deng was able to drop back and help out the defender who was marking her. She didn't manage a single shot on goal.

Just before half time Rob hit a pass to TJ on the wing. TJ beat his defender and took the ball forward at top speed. As he reached the goal line he hit a low cross back through the penalty area towards Tulsi. She was preparing to hit a volley when Deng reached out a long leg and hooked the ball out of the air. TJ couldn't believe he'd done it, and Tulsi groaned. Deng looked up and hit a pass that flew like a rocket towards Kelvin, the stocky Hillside striker. Kelvin took it on his chest and played a quick one-two with Krissy. Now he only had Jamie to beat, and Kelvin gave the Parkview keeper no chance with his low, hard shot. Hillside had pulled a goal back and now the score was 2–1 to Parkview. As the Hillside players celebrated, Mrs Singh blew the whistle for half time.

CHAPTER 7

'You were doing well,' Mr Wood said. 'And I don't think anyone could have stopped Deng doing that. It was a terrific piece of skill. You made a couple of excellent runs there, Tulsi. Let's see more of that this half.'

But when the second half got under way it was obvious to TJ that Tulsi was determined to stay as close to the penalty area as she could. 'Listen,' he said, jogging back for a word with Rob. 'Get the ball down the wing to me and I'll try to cross it onto Tulsi's head. I think she can beat that defender in the air.

49

But you can forget about her making fancy runs.'

Rob grinned. 'I guess you're right,' he said. 'Let's try it your way.'

Next time Rob had the ball he hit it long, towards the corner flag. TJ chased after it and reached it before Billy Martin, then he ran at the Hillside player, forcing him to back away. He turned inside, then outside, and hit a floating cross into the area. Tulsi jumped high. TJ saw her head rise above the defender's, but she wasn't quite tall enough, and the ball bounced away to the other side of the pitch.

Two minutes later, TJ tried again, but this time a different defender dived in front of Tulsi and headed the ball away. As it rolled out for a throw-in Mr Wood called Tulsi over.

'I'm taking you off, Tulsi,' he said. 'It's time to try something different. Ariyan, you saw those runs that Tulsi made in the first half. See if you can't do something like that.'

Ariyan ran onto the pitch and the game restarted. Every time Parkview had the ball Ariyan darted from side to side. He raced towards the goal. He stopped, turned, and sprinted for the corner flag. Then he dashed back towards his own half. Twice, Rob tried to pick him out with dangerous-looking passes, but by the time the ball arrived, Ariyan was somewhere else. 'Hey, Ariyan,' said TJ. 'Take it easy. You're confusing every-one.'

'Oh,' said Ariyan. 'I thought that was what I was supposed to do.'

'Sort of,' laughed TJ. 'Just not quite so much.'

And now, for the first time in the game, Parkview found themselves under real pressure. Deng seemed to be everywhere, tackling, dribbling, playing snappy clever little passes that put the Parkview defenders in trouble. Rodrigo and Tommy did their best to stop him, but then Krissy managed to lay the ball off to him on the edge of the penalty area and he stepped forward and shot savagely past Jamie.

'They've only had two shots,' Jamie complained, as he threw the ball to TJ. 'And they've scored from both of them. Now it's two–all.'

'Deng's too good,' said Tommy, shaking his head. 'When you try to tackle him, the ball's not there. It's like magic. Maybe I should stick to skateboarding.'

Once again, TJ thought of Danny. This was just the kind of situation where they needed him. He glanced over to where the rest of Year Six were watching. He could see Danny, pale-faced and intent. He obviously really cared about what was happening to the team, but he simply hadn't turned up to the last three training sessions. Still, there was nothing TJ could do about that now. 'You're doing great,' he said to Tommy. 'Even the best defenders at the PDC can't stop Deng when he's in this kind of mood.'

Parkview kicked off again, with the scores level. *I have to do something*, TJ thought, as Ariyan tapped the ball to him. He laid it back to Rafi and moved forward into the Hillside half, as Rafi slid the ball to Rob. Rob found TJ again with a pass that skimmed the surface of the grass. TJ killed the ball and turned. He saw Mrs Singh looking at her watch and he knew that there was no time to waste, so he ran directly at the goal. Billy Martin was in front of him, and the other defender was waiting too. There was no way through. Ariyan was racing out towards the corner flag, but Kelvin had chased back to mark him and the pass was impossible. Then TJ heard Rob's voice. 'Leave it to me! Go!'

TJ knew exactly what Rob would do, so he

shot forward like an arrow, bursting between the defenders, as Rob lifted the ball over their heads. He felt it coming over his shoulder, dropping right into his path and he hit a vicious dipping volley that fizzed past the goalkeeper before he had time to move. He'd scored a hat-trick! It was 3–2 to Parkview and it stayed that way until the end of the match.

'We'll beat you one day,' Krissy said ruefully to TJ when they shook hands after the game. 'I thought we were going to do it today until you scored that last goal.'

'You were good,' agreed TJ. 'And we're going to have to be a lot better than that if we want to win the Regional Tournament.'

'Maybe Deng could move to our school,' Rob said.

Deng grinned at Rob. The two midfield magicians had become good friends off the pitch. 'No way!' said Krissy, looking alarmed.

'Don't worry,' Deng said. 'I like it at Hillside. But I don't know why they haven't asked you to come to the PDC, Rob,' he went on. 'You should talk to your friend Marshall.'

Marshall Jones was a star at nearby Premier League side Wanderers. He was an old friend of Mr Wood's and he had given the Parkview team a lot of help.

'I don't think Marshall has much to do with the PDC,' TJ said. 'But I bet if Rob keeps playing that way then a scout will see him. I bet they'll ask him one day soon.'

'I don't think so,' said Rob.

'If I was as good as he is I'd make sure everyone knew it,' laughed Krissy, as Rob walked away.

'I don't think he actually knows just how good he is,' replied TJ.

Even though they'd won the match, TJ knew that it hadn't been a convincing victory. 'Those runs you made in the first half were amazing,' he said to Tulsi, as they waited for her mum when school was over. 'You should have kept doing them.'

'You're not the coach, are you?' snapped Tulsi. 'Just leave me alone, TJ.'

TJ opened his mouth to say something else, but Rob tugged at his arm. 'Not now,' he hissed. 'You'll just make it worse.'

'You were right,' TJ said to Rob a little later, as they walked home. 'It wasn't a good time to talk to Tulsi, but look – there's Danny. Let's have a word with him. I want to find out why he isn't coming to training.'

'You go if you like,' Rob said.

TJ glanced at him, then he remembered. When he'd first arrived at Parkview Danny and Rob had been enemies. 'He's a good tackler,' TJ said.

'I know,' replied Rob. 'But I don't have to like him, do I?'

CHAPTER 8

'Hey, Danny,' called TJ. 'Wait for me.'

Danny ignored him and kept on walking. TJ ran to catch him up. 'You haven't been to training,' he said.

'So?'

'We could have really used you today. You could have marked Deng.'

'You don't need me. You won anyway.'

'Only just. And we didn't deserve to, not really.'

'Look, I can't come, OK.'

'But why not?'

'Leave me alone, TJ. I've got things to do.'

Danny turned down the next street and walked off without looking back. Rob came up behind TJ. 'What did he say?'

'He wouldn't listen. I don't like it, Rob. Tulsi's in a terrible mood and if she doesn't watch out Mr Wood is going to drop her. Danny won't even try to get in the team. We started off so well today and then it all went wrong. What if that happens in the tournament?'

'Well,' said Rob seriously. 'All teams experience a dip in form at some point in the season. It's a well-known fact.'

TJ burst out laughing. 'Did you hear that on some TV programme?' he said.

Rob grinned. '*Match of the Day*,' he said. 'But it's true. And you just have to get on with it. All the best teams manage to win even when they're playing badly. It's what makes them great. And I've got a plan for Tulsi too.'

'Oh yeah?'

'When we go to see Wanderers next week I'm going to get her to watch their centre forward, Dwight Fanshawe, all the time. Then she'll see how much work he gets through when he hasn't got the ball.'

'I don't think anyone is going to tell Tulsi what to do,' said TJ. 'But I'm looking forward to the match. If they get to the Champions League final, will they give you tickets for that too?'

'That's what they told me,' Rob said.

As a birthday treat Jamie's dad had taken them to watch Wanderers play Milan in the Champions League. Rob had made a brilliant tactical suggestion and by an amazing stroke of luck the Wanderers manager had got to hear about it. Even more amazingly he had put Rob's plan into action, and Wanderers had won the match. Now Wanderers were in the knockout stage of the

Champions League and they had given Rob four tickets for every match they played, as a way of saying thank you.

The following Wednesday night Rob, Jamie, Tulsi and TJ all squashed into Rob's dad's car. When they reached the ground they were astonished to see Mr Wood waiting for them. 'I'm doing a few little jobs for the club on match days,' grinned Mr Wood, who was wearing his smartest suit again. 'And one of the first is to look after you lot. I thought I'd keep it a surprise.'

Mr Wood had been a promising young footballer at Wanderers when his career had been cut short by injury, and he had decided to become a teacher. But he was also a talented football coach, and Wanderers had recently offered him a job on the coaching staff. Luckily for TJ and his friends, Mr Wood had decided to stay at

Parkview School. 'You're going to like your seats,' Mr Wood told them. He led them up a flight of steps and TJ saw that they were right above the directors' box. 'Look!' said TJ. 'Isn't that . . . ?'

'It's the England manager,' breathed Rob.

'He's sitting three seats along from you,' said Mr Wood. 'Maybe you can give him some advice about tactics, Rob.'

'Well . . .' began Rob.

'I'm joking,' said Mr Wood quickly. 'These are your seats. And Phil here will sit with you. I've got other things I need to do. Have fun.'

They all knew Phil. He was a coach from the Wanderers Academy who had been to watch several of their matches. 'Any thoughts about tonight's game, Rob?' he asked, laughing, as they took their seats.

'I just hope we win,' Rob said. All around them people rose to their feet and applauded, as the teams walked out onto the field and the Champions League anthem rang out around the ground. Rob turned to Tulsi next to him. 'You should watch Dwight Fanshawe,' he said. 'It's what I do some-times. I just follow one player and do all their stats. Runs off the ball, passes received, passes made – all that stuff. It's really interesting.'

TJ, sitting the other side of Tulsi, waited for her to snap Rob's head off. She'd been very quiet on the journey to the ground.

'You watch him if you like,' she said. 'I'm not interested in stats, Rob. I came here for the football. I like Paco Sanchez and Mar-shall Jones. And there's great players in the Roma team too.'

'I just thought . . .'

'I know what you're trying to do, Rob,' said Tulsi. 'And it won't work, OK?'

The match kicked off, and Wanderers

went straight on to the attack. They had a 1–0 lead from the first leg in Rome, and it looked as if they were determined to score more goals. TJ decided to do what Rob had suggested, and he followed every move that Fanshawe made. It was a completely new way of watching a football match. When Roma had the ball Fanshawe retreated, harassing the Roma midfield players and making them pass more quickly, forcing them into mistakes. Then, whenever Wanderers regained possession, he began to move forward – and TJ could see that his movement always had a purpose.

A Wanderers defender won the ball and was quickly put under pressure by two Roma forwards, but he looked up and saw Fanshawe on the move and hit a long, high clearance. Fanshawe took the ball on his chest and shielded it from the defender who was marking him, then laid it neatly back to Paco Sanchez.

Sanchez played a pass to the other side of the field, but TJ kept watching Fanshawe. He moved forward towards the penalty area and the defender followed him closely. Just for a second the defender looked over to the left wing, where Marshall Jones was dribbling past a defender. Fanshawe checked his run and drifted away to his right. As Marshall's cross curled across the penalty area, always moving away from the goalkeeper, Fanshawe suddenly burst forward, rising above the helpless, out-of-position defender, and crashed the ball into the back of the net.

For the whole of the rest of the match, TJ couldn't stop watching Dwight Fanshawe. In the past his eyes had always been drawn most to the speed and skill of Marshall Jones, or the tricks and clever passing of

Paco Sanchez. He had never realized before just how much work Fanshawe did when he didn't have the ball. He didn't score again, but his tireless running created the space for Marshall to score two and Sanchez another as Wanderers thrashed Roma 4–0.

As the match neared its end, the PA system announced that Marshall Jones was the Man of the Match. 'I don't agree with that,' said Rob, as they stood up to applaud the players off the pitch. 'Dwight Fanshawe was terrific.'

'You're right,' agreed TJ. 'He never stopped running.'

'But it doesn't do him much good,' said Tulsi. 'Otherwise he would have won the award.'

'He's not bothered about the Man of the Match award,' Rob said. 'He was the best player on the pitch, and his manager knows it.'

'I thought so too,' said a deep voice behind them. The tall figure in the dark coat smiled briefly at them and then he was gone.

'That was him,' gasped Rob. 'The England manager.'

'You see,' TJ told Tulsi. 'Rob knows what he's talking about. He really does!'

CHAPTER 9

'You could play like that,' said TJ to Tulsi. 'I know you could.'

It was the following morning and he had arrived in the playground early, before anyone else. Tulsi was moodily banging a ball against the wall. 'I don't know what you're talking about,' she replied.

'Yes you do. You watched Dwight Fanshawe just like me and Rob did. Don't pretend you didn't.'

'But he knows what to do,' said Tulsi suddenly. 'And I don't.'

'Yes, you do. The runs you made on Friday were terrific.'

'I didn't know what I was doing, honestly. And anyway, no one passed to me.'

'That's not the point. Most of the time, no one passed to Dwight Fanshawe, but he made space for all the other players.'

'Why do I have to change the way I play? It was good enough before. I knew what I was doing. People passed to me and then I scored. It was dead simple.'

'That was when no one knew about you. You've scored so many goals that everyone knows how you play now. You could do it, Tulsi. I'm sure you could.'

'Hey, you two!' yelled a voice from above them. They looked up and saw an old lady looking down at them. A black cat was sitting on top of the wall beside her. 'Did one of you kick a ball into my garden last week?'

'I'm sorry,' said Tulsi. 'It was me. It was an accident.'

'Well, it's not good enough, young lady. You knocked over six flowerpots and they made a terrible mess. I've written to your head teacher and you'd better make sure you own up when he asks you about it. And make sure you don't kick any more footballs into my garden.'

'Tough luck,' said TJ. 'But I don't suppose Mr Burrows will mind too much. Not now football has made us famous. And you are our star striker after all.'

'Am I?' said Tulsi gloomily. 'I'm not so sure.'

'Hey, look,' said Jamie, running into the playground carrying a newspaper. He was closely followed by Rafi, Jamie and Rodrigo, all clutching copies of their own. 'We're in the paper,' Jamie said. 'All of us are. It's fantastic.'

TJ saw that more and more people were arriving now: little groups of mums and dads and children, some of the little ones squealing with excitement. 'Where?' said TJ. 'Let's see.'

Jamie opened the paper and saw a whole spread of photographs right across the centre pages. SCHOOL CHAMPIONS said the massive headline. 'See there,' said Jamie. 'There's you shooting, TJ, and there's me making a save.'

In another photograph Mr Wood and Mr Burrows were beaming at the camera and holding a copy of the inspectors' report on the school. 'It says our school is outstanding,' TJ said, reading the report. 'And it says how we're going to represent the district in the Regional Championships.'

'It's us,' said Leila. 'We're actually in the paper. Just about everyone. They've even put in a bit about Marshall Jones and Mr Wood.'

'Hey, Tulsi,' called Jamie. 'Where are you going?'

Tulsi didn't reply. 'It's because of this,' said Rob. 'There are pictures of all of us in the team, right? All of us except Tulsi.'

'She's not having a very good day,' TJ said, telling them about the old lady.

'She's not having a very good month, you mean,' said Jamie. 'We have to do something.'

'I've been trying,' said TJ. 'But nothing seems to work.'

Later that morning Mr Burrows came to the classroom to speak to Tulsi. 'I've had a complaint, young lady,' he said.

'It was an accident,' said Tulsi. 'I said I was sorry. I—'

Just for a moment TJ thought that Tulsi

was going to make things even worse, but Mr Burrows held up a hand. 'Quite right,' he said. 'I know you need to practise for the tournament, and I explained that to Mrs Barlow. I told her Mr Wood will take some of you round to weed her garden next week.'

Tulsi sat down again, but she still didn't look very happy. 'Now then,' Mr Burrows continued, 'I expect you've all seen the paper. Jolly good picture of me, I thought!'

Everyone laughed, but even that didn't cheer Tulsi up for long, and at break time she wouldn't even kick a ball around with her friends.

That night TJ's mum picked him up from school in the car. 'You're growing, TJ,' she said. 'Look at those trousers. We're going into town to get you some new ones.'

'Can we get new football boots as well?' TJ asked. 'Only I'll need them for the tournament. My old ones are getting too small.'

It was when they were coming out of the sports shop in the mall that TJ's mum said,

'Hey, look, TJ. Doesn't that boy go to your school?'

TJ peered over the balcony at the people milling around on the floor below. 'It's Danny,' he said. 'Hey, Danny! Up here!'

Danny looked up. 'Is that Danny's mum?' asked Mrs Wilson. 'She has got her hands full, hasn't she?'

Danny's mum was pushing a huge double buggy with a pair of screaming twins inside it. Danny was holding the hand of a toddler with a chocolate-covered face. TJ and his mum rode the escalator down to the next level and Mrs Wilson was soon busy admiring the twins. 'I'm Stacy,' said Danny's mum. 'Stacy Gray. This is Rosie, and these are the twins. They're six weeks old today.'

'And they never sleep,' said Danny gloomily.

'Really?' said TJ.

'Well, it seems like it,' Danny said. 'And when they wake up then Rosie wakes up too.'

Rosie was staring up at TJ, then she suddenly laughed and hid her face against Danny's legs. 'Danny's been great,' Mrs Gray told TJ's mum. 'My husband's away working abroad. Danny helps me feed the twins and he looks after Rosie. He's even learned to change their nappies.'

Danny's face went bright red. 'Mum!' he said. 'You don't have to tell everyone.'

'Is that why you don't come to training?' asked TJ.

'I told him I could manage,' said Mrs Gray. 'But he just wouldn't go.'

'I can't imagine TJ changing a baby's nappy,' said Mrs Wilson.

'Me, neither,' said TJ. And then he had an idea. 'Mum?' he said. 'I don't suppose . . .'

'What?'

'Maybe you could help Mrs Gray? We really need Danny in the team and—'

'I couldn't let you,' interrupted Danny's mum.

'No, wait,' said Mrs Wilson, who already seemed to have made friends with Mrs Gray. 'I'd love to give you a hand, Stacy. It wouldn't be any trouble, honestly. We could have a laugh together too.'

'Well, thanks,' replied Mrs Gray, smiling. 'That's brilliant. It'll be great for Danny to get out. It's training tomorrow, isn't it, boys?'

'Thanks, Mum,' said TJ. 'You'll come, won't you?' he asked Danny.

Danny hesitated, and looked at his mum.

'Sure,' he said finally. 'I'll be there.'

CHAPTER 10

'Don't tell them all I've been looking after the babies,' Danny said to TJ the next morning before school.

'Why not?'

'Just don't, that's all. Please.'

'Well, OK,' said TJ. 'But everyone would love those twins. They're well funny.'

'Not when they're both screaming at the same time, they're not,' said Danny. 'I bet your mum won't want to help out more than once.'

Everyone was surprised to see Danny at training that night. 'You can't just walk straight back into the team for the tournament,' Tulsi said to him.

'I know,' said Danny. 'I want to play football, that's all.'

'So where have you been?' asked Jamie.

'Busy,' replied Danny.

'Leave him alone,' said TJ. 'We should be warming up.'

They set off to jog around the edge of the field. Rob came up alongside TJ. 'Why do you want to be friends with Danny?' he said. 'You know he used to give me a hard time.'

'He doesn't any more, does he?' said TJ. Rob shook his head.

'I mean, maybe there was a reason he had a bad temper,' TJ continued. 'Perhaps it's not all his fault.'

Rob didn't reply.

TJ was certain that if he could just tell everyone all about Danny they'd like him a lot more. It was stupid. 'Well, anyway,' he said. 'Danny's a very good defender and we need him in the squad for the tournament, don't we?'

'Sure,' said Rob, and he put on a burst of speed that left TJ struggling to keep up.

Fifteen minutes into the training session Mr Wood called them all together. 'This next drill is all about penetrating defences,' he said. 'We're going to practise the wall pass, and we're going to practise at top speed. I want all of you to move as fast as you know how. TJ, Danny – come over here and we'll demonstrate.'

Mr Wood set up three cones close to the edge of the penalty area. 'These are defenders,' he told them. 'We'll have three groups working at this end of the pitch and three at the other end with Miss Berry. TJ, you run at the space to the left of the defender and you keep control of the ball with the outside of your front foot. You're trying to commit that defender. This one's only a cone, so it won't move.'

Everyone laughed. 'Then you fire the ball at Danny, who's waiting, half turned towards the goal. He'll be the wall and the ball will bounce off him. You run on and score. Ideally you shoot first time, but the most important thing is to get your shot on target. Show us how it's done.'

TJ put the ball down and Danny took up his position. TJ sprinted forward, trying to keep the ball as close to his feet as he could. As he approached the cone he touched the ball with his left foot, as if he was going to take it past the defender on that side, and then used his right foot to fire the ball at Danny. He raced into the penalty area and Danny's return pass fell perfectly for him to lash it into the net. There was a ripple of applause.

'That's good,' said Mr Wood. 'Now, TJ, you become the wall and Danny, you go to the back of the line. Tulsi, Rob and Jamie – you join them here. When everyone's had two goes on one cone, we'll swap round. Each cone gives you a different angle of attack on the goal. Remember, do it all as fast as you can.'

'I'll be rubbish at this,' laughed Jamie. 'Going fast isn't my thing.'

Tulsi didn't say anything at all. She was at the head of the line and TJ was the wall. She took the ball forward towards the cone and hit it to TJ, who bounced it back into her path. Tulsi raced after the ball, but somehow it got stuck under her foot, as she went to shoot. She stumbled, took a second touch and hit her shot just wide of the post.

'Bad luck,' said TJ, as he jogged past her to join the back of the line.

'It was a rubbish pass,' said Tulsi, as she got ready to be a wall for Rob, but TJ knew there had been nothing wrong with his pass.

Rob took off with the ball at his feet, dummied the defender and snapped his pass out to Tulsi. TJ knew at once that Tulsi's return pass was all wrong. It bounced up from her foot and flew towards Rob at waist height. Somehow, Rob twisted in the air, brought his knee up over the ball and volleyed it into the net. Then he jogged over to take his place as a wall.

It was Jamie's turn next. 'Watch me mess this up,' he said with a grin. His pass flew at Rob like a bullet, but Rob calmly took the pace off the ball and returned it expertly into Jamie's path. Jamie couldn't miss. 'I don't know which was better,' TJ said to Rob, as he rejoined the line, 'the volley or that pass. You've been practising again, haven't you?'

Rob grinned sheepishly. 'Every night,' he said. 'Against the wall in the back garden.'

'Great,' said TJ. 'Hey, Tulsi, did you see it?'

'Sure,' said Tulsi. 'Go on. It's you again.'

TJ hit another perfect one-two with Danny, then he was the wall again and Tulsi was rushing forward. She's trying too hard, thought TJ, as Tulsi hit her pass towards him. It was wild, and TJ had to move fast to his right and stretch out a leg just to reach the ball. Somehow he managed to play it back to Tulsi. She took a touch and planted the ball in the net.

As she turned to run back TJ saw an anxious look cross her face. She was looking towards the centre of the pitch where Mr

Wood was making a note on his clipboard.

'Don't worry,' TJ said. 'That was better.'

But TJ only had to look across at the other groups to know that there were at least ten other players who were making a better job of the drill than Tulsi was, and he could see that Tulsi knew that too.

At the end of the session Mr Wood announced the squad for their final warm-up match before the tournament. 'Jamie in goal. Defenders – Tommy, Rodrigo and Danny. Well done, Danny. Nice to have you back. Midfield – Rafi, Rob and Leila. Up front – TJ, Ebony and Ariyan. Tulsi, I know you've been in every squad so far, but I'm worried you look a bit tired. I think it might be best if you take a break for this one. We need you to be fresh for the tournament.'

'Fine,' muttered Tulsi under her breath. 'See if I care.'

CHAPTER 11

On Wednesday night Mr Wilson drove Jamie
and TJ to the Sports Centre where the Player
Development Centre was based. As usual,
Rob came with them so that he could go for
a run with TJ's dad on the Sports Centre's
running trail. 'So, who are you playing in this
friendly match then?' asked Mr Wilson.

'It's against the Sunday league team,
Meadow Green Wasps,' TJ told him. 'You
remember, we played them last term.
Leroy's their captain. Look, there he is now.'

TJ and Jamie knew Leroy well, because he
also attended the PDC. They got out of the

car and Rob took off with Mr Wilson to run ten kilometres. Leroy waved to Rob, as he ran past with TJ's dad. 'Your midfield genius,' he said to TJ and Jamie. 'I saw you all in the paper. But what happened to that girl? Your striker? There weren't any pictures of her. Has she left your school?'

'No,' said Jamie, shaking his head. 'But Mr Wood dropped her for our next match.'

'She was really good,' said Leroy, puzzled. 'What happened?'

'I wish I knew,' replied TJ. He turned to Jamie. 'Leroy's right, you know. We have to help Tulsi get back in the team.'

'Sure,' said Jamie. 'But what if she doesn't *want* to be in the team? Have you thought of that?'

That Sunday the Parkview team travelled in the minibus to the Wasps ground. Meadow Green Wasps had some of the best facilities in the whole area, and the place was buzzing with activity. Every pitch was occupied, and the home teams in their black and orange striped kit looked exactly like a swarm of angry wasps. As they were getting out of the minibus, TJ saw Tulsi. 'Great,' he said. 'You've come to watch.'

'I didn't want to,' she said irritably. 'Gran made me.'

'Hi, Mrs Patel,' said TJ. Tulsi's gran was wearing a big black Puffa jacket and a woolly hat. Strands of white hair sneaked out from the edges of her hat and her brown eyes twinkled when she saw the Parkview team.

'Hi, Jamie,' she said. 'Hello, Rodrigo. Hello, everyone. I'm really looking forward to this. Don't mind Tulsi. She's in one of her grumpy moods.'

Tulsi's gran was passionate about football. When they had held a World Food and

Football day at school Mrs Patel had played in goal for Tulsi's family team, and she'd been amazing. 'I've come to stay,' she said. 'I'll be here to support you in the tournament too. It's all very exciting.'

'Not for me,' said Tulsi. 'I think I might just give up football completely. I mean, if you're a boy you might have a chance to play for Wanderers one day, but I won't, will I?'

'Nonsense,' replied her gran. 'You won't give up if I have anything to do with it. You'll be back in the team in no time. I'm going to give you some of my special coaching.'

The others tried not to laugh. They could see from the expression on Tulsi's face that laughing wasn't a good idea. They ran off to get changed, and when they emerged from the dressing room Mr Wood was waiting for them. 'Listen,' he said. 'There's a TV crew here from the local station. They saw the story in the paper and they want to get some footage of you playing. I think they want to follow us at the Regional Tournament too. Just try to ignore them and concentrate on the football. I've told them they can't talk to any of you until after the match, and we'll be checking with your parents to make sure it's OK for you to be on TV.'

'They wouldn't dare to say no,' replied Jamie. 'Hey, it'll be like *Match of the Day*. One of us will have to be interviewed.'

'Maybe,' said Mr Wood. 'Now, this is our starting line-up. Tommy and Rodrigo, Rafi and Rob, then TJ and Ebony. Remember, I want to see movement, and lots of it. But not just running around for the sake of it,' he added, looking at Rafi. 'And I want us to pass the ball fast and accurately right from the start.'

Parkview Team Sheet

Attack
T.J. (captain) Ebony

Midfield
Rafi Rob

Defenders
Tommy Rodrigo

G.K.
Jamie

Subs
Danny Leila Ariyan

There was a sudden commotion near the entrance, and TJ caught sight of a flash of red in the car park. 'I don't believe it,' said Mr Wood. 'I told him not to come today.'

'It's Marshall,' said TJ happily, as the tall figure of Marshall Jones detached itself from the crowd and made its way towards them, waving. 'Why didn't you want him to come?'

'Too many distractions,' said Mr Wood. 'Still, I guess it might give you all a lift.'

'Hey, coach,' said Marshall, wrapping an

arm around his friend. 'I couldn't stay away. It's not often I get the chance to come and watch some football at the weekend. Hi, guys!'

'Hi, Marshall,' they all replied.

'We have to warm up,' Mr Wood told them, frowning slightly. It was then that TJ realized just how much it meant to Mr Wood that the Parkview team did well. 'We're wasting time,' Mr Wood continued. Then his face suddenly relaxed into a smile. 'You can carry that bag of balls, Marshall. You may as well do something useful as you're here. And the holdall.'

'OK, guvnor,' said Marshall with a grin. 'Be right there.'

When they reached the pitch the Wasps were already doing sprints. A big crowd of supporters had gathered along one touchline. TJ saw all of the dinner ladies with their blue sparkly pom-poms, and Mr Coggins brandishing a huge old-fashioned rattle. There were lots of mums and dads and grandparents too.

'It's a nice day,' said Jamie. 'I reckon they've all come out because it's sunny.'

'I don't think so,' said Marshall. 'You guys are getting famous. Newspapers. TV. You'll soon be more famous than me!'

'Off you go,' said Mr Wood to the team. 'TJ, you can be captain today. The ref is waiting.'

TJ felt suddenly nervous. He'd never been captain before. Leroy was waiting with the ref. 'Heads,' said TJ, and was relieved to see the queen's head glittering on the ground. 'We'll kick off.'

He shook hands with Leroy, then turned

and looked at his team. There was Jamie, filling the goal and looking unbeatable. Then Tommy and Rodrigo, both confident and smiling, and Rob with his usual look of fierce concentration. Rafi was bouncing up and down, ready to run for ever, and beside TJ even Ebony looked full of confidence although it was her first-ever start. Over on the touchline the subs were jogging up and down, keeping warm, ready to come on at any moment. It was a shame that Tulsi wasn't playing, but TJ felt really proud to be a member of this fantastic team. 'Come on!' he yelled. 'Let's show them what we can do, Parkview!'

The whistle blew, and he tapped the ball to Ebony.

CHAPTER 12

From his very first touch TJ knew that this game was going to be something special. Parkview lost the ball when Leroy made an interception, but Rafi won it back with a terrific tackle in midfield and slid it to Tommy who drilled an inch-perfect pass to Rob. Rob took the pace off the ball and slipped effortlessly away from his marker before hitting another fine pass to Ebony's feet.

Rob's pass was so perfectly weighted that Ebony was able to play the ball first time to TJ, who instantly moved forward at pace, wrong-footing the defender. TJ touched the ball forward with the outside of his right foot, as the defender backed away uncertainly. Was TJ about to go outside him? Was it a bluff? TJ saw the defender make his move. He'd decided TJ was going outside and he lunged into a tackle. TJ opened his body and played a firm pass inside the defender with the inside of his back foot. He jumped over the defender's leg and sprinted away down the wing. Ebony had played the return pass perfectly, just as he'd known she would. And now she had turned and was racing into the penalty area, taking a defender with her.

Out of the corner of his eye, TJ saw Rob making a run. He was coming at top speed, heading for the empty space just outside the area that Ebony's run had created. TJ knew the moment the ball left his foot that he couldn't have hit it better. The pass had just enough pace on it to carry it perfectly into Rob's path. He didn't even have to break his stride, as he curled his shot expertly just inside the post.

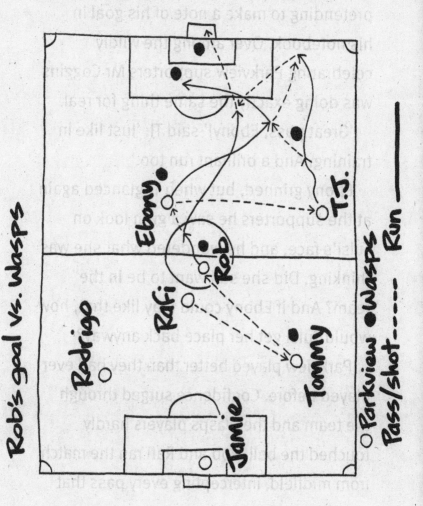

Rob's goal vs. Wasps

Rodrigo

Jamie

Rafi

Rob

Ebony

Tommy

T.J.

○ Parkview ● Wasps

Pass/shot ----- Run ──────

Rob had been practising his celebration. He held his hand in front of his face and pretended to write on it. TJ laughed, as he ran up to congratulate him. Rob was pretending to make a note of his goal in his notebook. Over among the wildly celebrating Parkview supporters Mr Coggins was doing exactly the same thing for real.

'Great pass, Ebony!' said TJ. 'Just like in training. And a brilliant run too.'

Ebony grinned, but when TJ glanced again at the supporters he saw a grim look on Tulsi's face, and he wondered what she was thinking. Did she still want to be in the team? And if Ebony could play like that, how would Tulsi get her place back anyway?

Parkview played better than they had ever played before. Confidence surged through the team and the Wasps players hardly touched the ball. Rob and Rafi ran the match from midfield, intercepting every pass that

Wasps played forward and then making probing passes of their own into the Wasps half. TJ scored with a header when Ebony chipped the ball back across the six-yard-box after Rob had put her through. Then TJ laid on a goal for Ebony when she created space for herself with a clever, twisting run. Ebony grabbed a second goal when the keeper dropped a cross from Rafi and she pounced quickly to bundle the ball into the net.

And with the final kick of the first half TJ scored his second. Rob hit the ball towards Ebony, as TJ was running behind her. She stepped over it, taking two defenders out of the game and wrong-footing the keeper, as the ball ran through to TJ. He had never scored an easier goal.

The whole team surrounded Ebony and TJ, as they walked off the pitch. They were all buzzing with excitement, and even Mr Wood didn't try to hide how pleased he was. 'You were terrific,' he said. 'And, Ebony, you fitted in as if you've been playing in the team all your life. Well done, everyone. Five great goals!'

TJ looked over at the far side and saw the TV cameraman filming the dinner ladies going through their routine. Over by the dressing rooms the reporter was talking to Marshall, surrounded by a small group of Marshall's fans. He couldn't see Tulsi and her gran anywhere. 'Hey, TJ,' said Mr Wood. 'Did you hear what I said?'

'Sorry, Mr Wood.'

'This is a perfect chance to give our subs a proper run-out. So you're coming off, TJ, and Ariyan will play up front with Ebony. Leila, you can take Rob's place, and Danny, you'll come on for Tommy. Everyone happy? Let's see if we can score another five this half!'

'Did you see where Tulsi went?' TJ asked Rob. They were watching from the touchline, as the rearranged Parkview team ran out for the second half.

'There,' said Rob. 'Over in the car park.'

Even from this far away TJ could see that Tulsi and her gran were arguing. 'I bet she feels terrible,' Rob said. 'Ebony's doing really well.'

There was a roar from the crowd. Rob and TJ turned back to the pitch in time to see Ebony celebrating yet another goal. 'It's her hat-trick,' said TJ, clapping as hard as anyone.

Parkview were still on top, but in the second half the defence had some real work to do at last. With Rob no longer running the midfield Parkview couldn't manage to keep hold of the ball quite so well, and Leroy began to create some dangerous attacks. But when he did, Danny and Rodrigo snuffed out all of them except one, when Jamie tipped the ball over the bar after Leroy's fierce drive.

'Danny's good,' Rob said grudgingly, as Parkview walked off the field at the final whistle having won 6–0. 'You were right. In the tournament we're going to need him. But you know what? I still think we need Tulsi too. We can't let her stop playing football.'

'But she might not even get in the squad,' TJ said. 'You saw how well we played. Mr

Wood is bound to pick the same squad again, isn't he?'

'Ebony is small,' Rob said. 'And so are you and Ariyan. What if we're up against a team with really big defenders? We'll need a big strong striker like Tulsi.'

'You're right,' said TJ thoughtfully. 'And she isn't *always* selfish with the ball. Remember those runs she made in the last game against Hillside? They were brilliant. If she'd just do more of that . . .'

'I know,' replied Rob. 'But getting her to do it, that's the problem.'

CHAPTER 13

TJ and Rob walked over to join the rest of the team. Marshall was shaking hands with everyone. 'You've got a fantastic squad here, Johnny,' he said to Mr Wood. 'That's the best I've seen you play,' he said to everyone. 'And that's even with your star striker missing. Where is she?'

'You mean Tulsi?' said Mr Wood. 'Well . . .'

'Excuse me, Mr Wood.' Maggie Burnside, the TV presenter, pushed through the Parkview squad with the cameraman and sound man behind her. 'You said we could talk to one of the children after the game? And if it would be great if we could have you at the same time, Marshall,' she simpered.

Marshall held up a hand. 'This is all about the kids,' he said. 'And their outstanding coach, of course. I'd rather not, thanks.'

The presenter's face wrinkled with disappointment. Her make-up was like an orange mask and her hair was impossibly perfect. 'Well, then,' she said. 'We'd like to interview the star of the match. The hat-trick heroine we're calling her.' She pointed her finger at Ebony. 'We've got some terrific footage of your goals, so come and tell us how you did it.'

They all watched, as Maggie Burnside took a nervous Ebony to one side. 'How does it feel to be the star of such a successful team?' she asked.

Ebony blushed. 'Oh, well, I'm not the

star,' she said. 'Honestly.'

'You looked like a star to me. You scored a hat-trick.'

'I mean . . . it wasn't just me . . . it was everyone . . .'

'You're too modest. You're the one who scored the goals. And you're playing in a big tournament soon, I hear. I expect you'll score lots of goals there too.'

Ebony shuffled her feet and looked embarrassed. 'I hope so,' she said. 'But I might not be in the team. There's lots of really good players at our school.'

But the TV presenter wasn't really listening.

'I'm sorry, everyone,' Ebony said, as the TV crew walked away. 'I didn't know what to say.'

'You did fine,' said Mr Wood. 'Couldn't have been better. Hello, Phil. I didn't see you arrive.'

They all turned to look at the newcomer. Phil, the Wanderers Academy coach, often watched youth football matches, looking for talented young players. 'Terrific perform-ance, everyone,' he said. 'As good as I've seen. You keep discovering new players, Johnny,' he continued, with a glance at Rob. 'I knew this lad was a tactical genius, but I didn't know he actually played football.'

'I didn't before,' said Rob. 'I mean, before Mr Wood came back.'

Phil nodded. 'Well, that was a really great team performance,' he said. 'It was a pleasure to watch.'

On the minibus on the way back to school the team discussed Phil's comments excitedly. 'Maybe we'll all play for Wanderers one day,' said Rafi.

'I won't,' said Ebony.

'Me neither,' said Leila, 'and Tulsi won't either.'

'Don't be so sure,' Mr Wood called from the front seat. 'Marshall tells me that Wanderers are thinking about a Ladies Team, and they're planning a Girls' Academy too. So don't give up hope just yet.'

TJ had only just finished his lunch that same afternoon when there was a knock on the door. His sister Lou answered it and came back into the room with Jamie, Rafi and Rob behind her. 'Any more coming in?' asked TJ's dad, peering round Jamie to see.

'We just wanted to talk to TJ,' Jamie said, with an envious look at the bowl of tropical fruit salad in the middle of the table. TJ's mum saw where he was looking. 'You still have an appetite then, Jamie,' she laughed. 'Go on, boys. Have some if you like. We've finished.'

The boys tucked in gratefully. 'What's all this about then?' asked TJ's dad.

'It's Tulsi,' said Jamie. 'We have to get her back in the team but it seems almost like she's not interested any more. She's even started talking about giving up football.'

'So we're going to tell her about the Girls' Academy,' Rob said. 'They might be starting one at Wanderers.'

'I can't believe Tulsi would want to give up football,' said TJ's mum. 'She was the keenest of all of you.'

'But it's true,' said TJ. 'And it must be strange if you're a girl and you love playing football but you know you won't ever be able to play in the Champions League like Marshall does. Like we might one day.'

'Hey,' said TJ's mum. 'That's a very long speech, TJ. But you're right. It must be tough for Tulsi.'

'There *is* a women's World Cup,' said Lou. 'And there's the Olympics. And quite a lot of Premier League sides have ladies' teams,

Centres of Excellence for Women and Girls in England.

There are <u>52</u> of them!
Lots of them are associated with Premier League clubs. There's an FA Women's Premier League too.

Centres of Excellence have under 10s, under 12s, under 14s and under 16s.

The Centres run for between 24 and 30 weeks each year and they usually have trials in June. You have to live within 90 minutes travelling time to join.

Registered players have at least two training sessions a week. One is at least 90 minutes and the other is at least an hour. There are matches on Saturday too, but you only play against teams from other Centres of Excellence.

don't they?'

'You're right,' said TJ. 'Thanks, Lou. We'll tell her that too. We're going to try to get her to come to the park with her gran this afternoon. We can have a kickabout for fun like we used to. She can't say no to that. And then we can tell her about the Academy.'

But . . .

'I'm sorry,' said Tulsi's mum, when they arrived at her house. 'She's not feeling well. She's lying down in her room.'

'No, she's not,' said Tulsi's gran, peering over her daughter's shoulder at Tulsi's friends. 'She's sulking, that's what she's doing.'

'We thought she might want to come to the park,' Rob said. 'Just to kick a ball around.'

'And we've got some news,' added TJ. 'Wanderers are going to have an Academy for girls. Can you tell her?'

A few minutes later Mrs Patel came downstairs with Tulsi. Anyone could see Tulsi had been crying.

'We're both coming,' said Tulsi's gran. 'I'll just change into my tracksuit and trainers.'

'Well?' asked Tulsi, as they walked to the park. 'Is it true? Wanderers are really going to have an Academy for girls?'

'Mr Wood only said they're talking about it,' replied TJ. 'But he made it sound as if they're serious. Hey, look. There's six of us. We can play three against three with rush goalies. You'll play, Mrs Patel, won't you?'

'You think I came along to watch?' said Tulsi's gran. 'No fear! How about me, Tulsi and Rob against the rest of you?'

'OK,' said TJ. 'This should be good!'

CHAPTER 14

'I'll go up front, then,' said Tulsi.

'Are you mad?' said her gran. 'It's three against three with rush goalies. I'm not as young as I was. I can't be running up and down all the time. No, we can't have set positions. We have to play total football, like the famous Dutch team did in the nineteen-seventies. Everyone plays everywhere. We move around and fool the opposition.'

'I don't know what you're talking about, Gran. And we'd better decide who's going in goal, because here they come.'

'You go in,' yelled Mrs Patel. 'Go on! Get

back!'

Tulsi sprinted back to guard the bench that was acting as their goal. She was just in time to put out a foot and stop TJ's shot.

'Great!' shouted her gran, darting forward suddenly. 'Now give it to me! Come on!'

TJ couldn't help laughing. Mrs Patel was taking the whole thing very seriously. But when she took the ball out of the air easily with her left foot and then turned and hit an instant pass to Rob, TJ's jaw dropped. He hadn't expected Tulsi's gran to be able to do something like that, even though he'd seen her make some great saves when she'd played in goal during the Parkview mini-World Cup. 'Get to Rob,' he called to Rafi. 'I'll mark Mrs Patel.'

TJ positioned himself to stop Mrs Patel passing. She looked up and saw Tulsi hanging back, guarding the goal. 'Tulsi,' she said. 'You have to move, girl. Just like you would in a match. You make the run and I lay it on for you to shoot. Or you make a run so that Rafi has to leave Rob and mark you, and then I pass to Rob.'

For a moment TJ thought that Tulsi was going to lose her temper. But then she jogged forward. 'Come on then, Gran. Give it here.'

Mrs Patel passed to Tulsi, who saw Rob sprint a few paces forward, then turn and check back, fooling Rafi for a second. Tulsi hit the ball towards him and Rob instantly played it into empty space. The space didn't stay empty for long. Mrs Patel had continued her run after passing to Tulsi. She latched onto Rob's pass and hit a low shot at the goal. Jamie dived and saved it.

'You could be in our school team, Mrs Patel,' he said with a grin, as he stood up. 'That was a fantastic run!'

Tulsi was staring at her gran. 'That was awesome, Gran,' she said.

'It was nothing,' Mrs Patel replied. 'You can do the same thing. I've seen you do it.'

'When?' demanded Tulsi.

'When you were a little girl. When you used to come and stay with me. We used to play with the other children in the park and you were a natural footballer. You knew just where to move and what to do.'

'Are you sure?' asked Tulsi. 'Really?'

'Really,' said her gran. 'And you can still do it, I bet. All you need is a little more confidence. And forget about all this goal-hanging nonsense!'

Jamie dribbled the ball forward. He passed to TJ who was wondering whether Tulsi was going to get sulky again. She hated being called a goalhanger. But now, suddenly she began to play. She ran to TJ, trying to block his pass. TJ dragged the ball back and somehow squeezed it out to Rafi, but Mrs Patel tackled Rafi quickly and efficiently and then tapped the ball to Rob, who played a clever chip forward for Tulsi to chase.

TJ refused to let her get away from him. He gained half a metre on her. Enough to stop her shooting, but not enough to stop her taking him completely by surprise. She back-heeled the ball and Rob ran onto it and slammed a shot at Jamie's goal. This time Jamie had no chance and the ball flashed between the two trees and ran away into the distance. 'I told you,' said Tulsi's gran, exchanging high-fives with her. 'You're as good as anyone when you try. I bet when they open that Academy for girls you'll be the first one through the door.'

'Hey!' called a voice from the park gates. 'They're here!'

Krissy Barton swooped down the path

towards them on her bike, followed by Kelvin and Deng. 'Great!' she said, dumping her bike on the ground. 'We'll give you a game.'

'It's not fair sides,' said Tulsi. 'You'd better have my gran.'

'And Rafi too,' said TJ, seeing the doubtful look in Krissy's eyes. 'Go on. Five against four. You can't say that's not fair. But your goalie has to stay in goal.'

Rafi went in goal for the Hillsiders. 'But you'd better try properly,' Krissy warned him. 'No letting shots in to help your mates.'

It was a very even match. Mrs Patel and Deng understood each other right from the start, playing clever passes that forced Rob, Tulsi, TJ and Jamie to tear around trying to intercept the ball. And all the time the Hillsiders were looking for a chance to catch Jamie out of his goal and hit a long-range shot.

Then Jamie tackled Kelvin and his pass found Rob. Rob turned away from Deng and both TJ and Tulsi were calling for it. Rob slid a pass to Tulsi and ran for the return. When it came, he flicked the ball on to TJ, who drilled it, first time, back to Tulsi. She could see the goal, and she could see Rafi bouncing up and down, waiting for her shot. But her head was up and she could see everything that was happening around her. TJ was making a darting run towards the goal. Rob had checked his own run and made himself some space. And there was Jamie thundering up from the back. She laid the ball sideways, right into Jamie's path, and he slammed it into the goal.

'Oh, very good, Tulsi!' said her gran. 'You see how easy it is?'

'Hey!' said Krissy. 'Whose side are you on, Mrs Patel?'

'Our side of course,' said Mrs Patel. 'Come

on. It's only one–nil.'

They played on until the sun began to go down behind the houses on the far side of the park. TJ thought that he had never enjoyed playing football so much. 'Good luck in the tournament,' Krissy said to Tulsi, as they walked out of the park together.

'Thanks,' replied Tulsi. 'But I might not even be playing. I have to get back in the team first, and it's not going to be easy.'

CHAPTER 15

On Monday night TJ's family gathered in the living room to watch the local news on TV.

'This should be good,' said TJ's dad. 'You were all amazing yesterday. Your first time on TV, TJ!'

'Don't, Dad,' said Lou. 'He's big-headed enough already.'

'I'm not,' said TJ. 'Just because *you've* never been on TV.'

'Be quiet, all of you,' said TJ's mum. 'It's starting.'

Maggie Burnside's orange face filled the screen. She was standing outside Parkview

School and Mr Burrows was beside her with a huge smile on his face. 'Inspectors say that this is an outstanding school,' Maggie Burnside said. 'And the most outstanding thing about it is its under-eleven football team. Tell us about the team, Mr Burrows.'

'Er, well . . . It all began with Mr Wood,' Mr Burrows said. 'He came to our school as a temporary teacher at the start of the year, and it turns out he's a bit of a whiz at football coaching.'

'Which isn't surprising when you realize that he was a promising young footballer at Wanderers,' Maggie Burnside said. 'We have some footage of Johnny Wood in action playing for England's under-eighteen side. If you look closely you might also spot current Wanderers star, Marshall Jones.'

'There!' exclaimed TJ. 'That's Mr Wood!'

A tall, skinny boy controlled the ball on the screen and played a pass elegantly out to the right wing. 'And that's Marshall,' said Lou. 'He looks great!'

'They're just kids,' said TJ's mum. 'Look at them, TJ. They're not much older than you.'

'I know,' said TJ, who had been thinking the same thing. But now the screen changed. Maggie Burnside was talking to the camera, and in the background the Parkview dinner ladies were chanting and dancing. 'Parkview have already won their District Championship this year,' the presenter said. 'And they've won the Inter-Schools Cup too. This weekend they'll be off to the Regional Championship. We've come to their final warm-up match to see for ourselves just how good they are.'

There was a long shot of the match in progress. 'There you are, TJ,' said his brother Joey. 'Over there on the wing. And there's Jamie.'

Then Ebony filled the screen, scoring her

first goal, followed by a shot of the keeper dropping the ball and Ebony sliding home her second. Finally they saw Ebony complete her hat-trick, before the camera cut back to Maggie Burnside interviewing her.

'That's not right,' said Joey. 'Anyone would think Ebony was the only person in the team.'

'You're the one who scored the goals,' Maggie Burnside was saying. 'And you're playing in a big tournament soon, I hear. I expect you'll score lots of goals there too.'

'I hope so,' replied Ebony.

'That was Ebony Green,' Maggie Burnside said. 'Hat-trick heroine of Parkview School. And this is Maggie Burnside, handing you back to the studio.'

There was silence in the Wilsons' living room. 'It's not Ebony's fault,' TJ said. 'I mean, it is amazing that she scored a hat-trick in her first match.'

'Just like you, you mean?' smiled his mum. 'I suppose you're right. But I still think it's a shame there was nothing about all the work everyone did, mending the football pitch and painting and decorating and the World Food day, and the school dinners . . .'

'It's OK, Mum,' TJ said. But he couldn't help feeling disappointed. And he knew that Tulsi was going to be more annoyed than anyone.

He was right. When he got to school the next day Tulsi was hopping mad. 'How could she?' she was saying to Jamie in the play-ground. 'It was just her first full game, and she wouldn't have scored any of those goals if it hadn't been for the rest of you.'

'It wasn't really like that. . .' Jamie began.

But Tulsi interrupted. 'I'm going to tell her

what I think,' she said angrily. 'There she is now.'

'Don't,' said Jamie. 'She didn't do anything wrong.'

But it was too late to stop Tulsi. She was already standing in front of Ebony. 'You shouldn't have talked to them,' she said. 'You could have let Jamie do it, or TJ, or . . . or anybody.'

'I know,' said Ebony tearfully. 'I'm really sorry. I'm going to tell Mr Wood I don't want to be in the team any more.'

Tulsi had her mouth open to say more things to Ebony, but now she stopped. 'You can't,' Jamie told Ebony. 'You played great. We need you in the tournament, just like we need Tulsi.'

'He's right,' said TJ. 'We're going to need all our best players. We'll be playing against some of the best teams in the country.'

'I can't do it,' said Ebony. 'Not after that.

Everyone thinks I wanted to be the one they took pictures of, but I didn't.'

Ebony walked miserably into school.

'You'll have to talk to her,' Jamie said to Tulsi. 'She'll listen to you. She was so good on Sunday. We need her in the squad.'

'What, instead of me?' asked Tulsi.

'No way,' said TJ. 'You know none of us will play every game in the tournament. Except Jamie in goal, unless he gets injured. We need Ebony to play.'

But when school ended and everyone went to fetch their football kit Tulsi still hadn't said anything to Ebony. Ebony collected her bag and headed for the exit.

'Tulsi,' said TJ. 'You have to. Go and talk to her. It's not fair, you know it isn't.'

Tulsi hesitated, then she sighed and dropped her bag on the floor. She ran out of the door and TJ saw her catch up with Ebony by the school gate. They talked for a few moments, then they both turned and walked back into school.

'At last,' said TJ. 'Now maybe we can get on with training.'

'And after all that,' said Rob, 'we'd better hope that Tulsi can still remember how to play the way she did in the park.'

'I think she might,' said TJ with a grin. 'It looks like her personal coach has come along to give her some help. Hi, Mrs Patel.'

Tulsi's gran gave them a big wave, as they ran onto the field. 'Knock 'em dead, Tulsi,' she yelled, with a wave of her umbrella.

CHAPTER 16

'First of all,' Mr Wood said when they'd finished their warm-ups, 'I hope none of you paid any attention to that TV report. Ebony played very well, but it was a team performance, and that's what we'll need to win the tournament. I've arranged some fixtures for our B team and I'll be choosing that team today as well. So you've all got plenty to work for. Now, take a ball with your partner and work in a ten-metre square. One of you dribbles and shields the ball, the other one tries to win it. Dead simple. Off you go.'

TJ was working with Rob. 'We do this sort of thing on the playground all the time,' said TJ. 'Why's he making us do it now?'

'Maybe because you're rubbish at it,' said Rob, sneaking a foot around TJ's defences and tapping the ball away from him. 'Go on, then, get it off me.'

Rob hunched himself over the ball like a crab. Then, when TJ committed himself and tried to tackle him, Rob flicked the ball up onto his foot and over TJ's head. 'I've been wanting to try that for ages,' Rob said, laughing. 'I saw Paco Sanchez doing it on the Internet. What do you think?'

'I think you should let me have a turn at dribbling,' TJ said, as Rob fended him off expertly once again.

'You give up then?' said Rob. 'You're admitting I'm better than you?'

Rob took his eye off the ball for a second and TJ darted in and stole it away. 'Ha!'

he said. 'I fooled you.'

They were still laughing when Mr Wood called them together. 'It's an important skill,' he said. 'I know I've coached you to move the ball quickly, but there are lots of times when you just need to hold onto it. We'll be playing against top teams and in a close game it's crucial that you can keep the ball and give other players a chance to find space for you to make a pass. Now, before we play five-a-side we'll have a little game of pig-in-the-middle. Three circles, two players in the middle of each, and you all have to play the ball first time with your weaker foot. We'll be watching, so no cheating. Oh, and if you're in the middle when my whistle blows you have to show us your best dance move for ten seconds!'

By the time they finished the game, everyone was laughing, and TJ had learned at least ten dance moves he would never have thought of. 'Some of those moves were seriously bad,' laughed Rafi, as Mr Wood organized them into teams.

'Yeah, but did you see Jamie? He can actually dance!'

'Maybe he should do it in a match,' replied Rafi. 'When the other team are taking a penalty. That would really put them off!'

'Get a move on, you two,' called Mr Wood. 'You're on this pitch here with Tommy and Danny, and Jamie in goal. You're the Greens.'

'Hey!' said TJ. 'This should be fun.'

'You can play against this lot,' Mr Wood continued. 'Ebony, Tulsi, Leila, Rob. Diane – you go in goal.'

Rob laughed and pulled on a blue bib.

'You know what?' he said to TJ. 'I reckon we can beat you.'

'Hi, TJ,' called a girl's voice from the other

side of the fence. TJ looked up and saw his sister Lou. She was with Matt, Jamie's brother. TJ suddenly felt nervous. If he got beaten by a team with four girls in it, Lou would never stop going on about it. Not ever. And he knew that the girls were good. With Rob laying on passes for them they might even be *very* good.

Tulsi kicked off, and Ebony played the ball back to Rob. Tommy went to tackle him, but even Tommy wasn't going to get the ball off Rob. He turned away and laid the ball back to Leila, who curved a pass forward to Ebony. She took the ball in her stride and then pulled it back to Tulsi in midfield. TJ tried to get a tackle in, but Tulsi had already released the ball back to Rob, and . . .

TJ couldn't believe it. He'd lost Tulsi! One moment she'd been there, and now . . . Where was she? Then he looked round and saw her. At the same moment he saw the ball flash past him, saw Tulsi hit it first time, and almost at the same instant, saw it crash into the back of the net.

Mr Wood stood on the touchline and applauded. 'Great teamwork, Blues!' he said. 'Keep it up! Let's see you come back at them, Greens.'

'We can't lose,' TJ hissed at Rafi. 'My sister's watching.'

'You'd better do something brilliant, then,' grinned Rafi. Jamie rolled the ball out to Danny, and then it was at TJ's feet. He gave it inside to Rafi and set off on a run down the wing, but as he chased after Rafi's return pass he was astonished to see Tulsi running beside him. He just managed to reach the ball first, but he couldn't get a cross in. He turned and shielded the ball from Tulsi, desperately looking for someone to pass to. Rafi and Tommy both called for it, but they were both marked. *I have to get past her*, thought TJ, and he tried to fool Tulsi with a swerve. But she knew him too well. She took the ball away from him and snapped off a pass to Rob, who instantly hit it upfield into the path of Ebony's curving run. Jamie managed to save her shot, but only just. At the end of the game the score was still 1–0 to the Blues.

'What's up, TJ?' Rob asked him, as they put the equipment away. 'You're not still worrying about being beaten by girls.'

'No,' replied TJ. 'And they had you on their side anyway. That makes a big difference.'

'What then?'

'Tulsi and Ebony are both fantastic. They played really well together, especially with you giving them passes.'

'So?'

'Well, I'd been thinking that if Tulsi got back in the squad then some of the time I'd play up front with Tulsi, and sometimes with

Ebony. But there was another possibility that I hadn't thought of. Mr Wood might want Tulsi to play up front with Ebony. Some games I might not even play at all.' He got changed in silence. *It could actually happen*, he thought. *Even if I'm playing well Mr Wood might decide it's better to play the others. He might drop me.*

And suddenly, for the first time, he really understood how Tulsi had been feeling.

CHAPTER 17

When TJ left school after training his sister
was waiting for him. 'Hey, TJ,' she said, 'I'll
walk home with you.'

TJ groaned. He knew he couldn't stop her.
When Lou decided to do something then
she did it, whether you liked it or not. 'Hi,
Rob,' she said, as he joined them. 'Nice
work with those girls. Did they all get in the
team?'

'Tulsi, Ebony and Leila did. Diane's goalkeeper in the B team. Mr Wood's entered
them into a league. Actually, the B team

could probably beat most other teams around here.'

'So, who else is in the squad?' demanded Lou. 'I want to hear it first!'

'Jamie in goal,' replied Rob with a grin. 'Tommy, Rodrigo and Danny in defence. You were right about Danny, TJ. He makes a lot of tackles.'

'Danny got in!' said Lou. 'That's great. You should see those little twins, Rob. They are so cool. I went round to Danny's house with Mum the other day.'

'What twins?' asked Rob.

'He's got little sisters,' said Lou. 'He's been looking after them lots. That's why he wasn't going to training. And they were keeping him up at night too, and . . .'

'And he told me not to tell anyone,' TJ said, with a look at his sister.

'So, who else is in the team then?' said Lou after a pause.

'Well, there's Rafi in midfield and me and TJ and that's it,' said Rob.

'You're not saying much, TJ,' Lou said.

'He's worrying about his place in the team.'

'No way! Is that true, TJ?'

TJ nodded. 'You saw Ebony playing with Tulsi. Mr Wood could easily play both of them up front. Why not?'

'You are a fool, little bro,' his sister told him. 'You've just spent ages helping Tulsi get back in the team because you know you need a strong squad for this tournament. And now you've got a strong squad, here you are moaning about it.'

'You're right,' replied TJ. 'I suppose I'm just a bit nervous, that's all.'

'You should be,' Lou said, smiling. 'We're all coming to watch and I'm expecting something big.'

*

The tournament was taking place on Saturday in a big city nearly a hundred miles away. The squad were going to travel there on Friday afternoon with Mr Wood and Miss Berry, leaving school at lunch time and staying the night in a Youth Centre close to the ground. On Friday morning TJ was awake long before his alarm went off. He had dreamed in the night that they had reached the final, and Ebony had scored a hat-trick. He couldn't remember if he'd been playing or not.

He got up and checked his kit again, then looked at his overnight bag. He had never spent the night in a strange place on his own before. Well, he knew he wouldn't be on his own, but his mum and dad wouldn't be there until the next day, or his gran either. He told himself he was being stupid. It was only one night. He could guess what Lou would say.

His alarm went off, and the day began. They were eating breakfast when they heard the clatter of the letterbox. TJ's dad came back into the kitchen with a bundle of letters in his hand. He was reading one of them.

'What is it?' asked TJ's mum. 'I know that look. It's something important, isn't it?'

'No, no,' said Mr Wilson. 'We have to get TJ off on his big adventure. I'll tell you about it later. Now then, TJ, are you ready? Have a good trip. We'll see you at the ground tomorrow.'

'Here,' said his mum, squeezing a large plastic box into the top of one of his bags. 'Snacks for the journey,' she said, giving him a kiss. 'Good luck, love.'

'Has anyone seen Danny?' Mr Wood asked them, when he had finished calling the register. 'TJ, you're his friend, aren't you?'

'He's not here,' TJ said. 'Maybe he's ill.'

Mr Wood looked worried. 'I hope not,' he said. 'It's really too late to arrange for anyone to take his place. I'll get the office to call home and see if we can find out what's happened. I'm sure he'll be here by break time.'

But at morning break there was still no sign of Danny. It wasn't until the minibus was actually pulling out of the school gate that TJ saw him running down the road towards them with two bags bouncing awkwardly against his side. 'Stop!' called TJ to Mr Wood. 'Wait!'

'I'm really sorry,' Danny gasped, as Miss Berry opened the side door and let him into the bus.

'OK, Danny,' laughed Miss Berry. 'You made it. That's the main thing. Right, everyone. We're on our way at last.'

'Are you OK?' TJ asked, as Danny sat quietly in the seat in front of him, but Danny shook his head and didn't reply and TJ was soon busy talking to the rest of his excited team-mates.

There were five other teams staying at the Youth Centre that night. By the time the Parkview minibus arrived after a long hold-up on the motorway all the other teams were already eating in the canteen. TJ and Rob collected a big plateful of sausage and mash and sat at a table where a noisy conversation was going on.

'You should have seen it,' a tall boy with curly black hair was saying. 'We were playing the Manchester United Academy and Bazza was just too good for them. Well, we all were, but Bazza got the goals.'

He patted the boy next to him on the head. The boy grinned behind his glasses.

'I'm glad I'm not the only one who wears them,' Rob muttered to TJ.

'They all play for Academies at big clubs

as well as their school teams,' whispered TJ. 'They must all be brilliant.'

'Who are you lot?' asked the curly-haired boy. 'Where are you from?'

'Parkview School,' said TJ.

'Never heard of them. Are any of you playing for an Academy?'

TJ shook his head. 'I'd like to, though,' he said awkwardly, trying to be friendly. 'Me and Jamie go to the Wanderers Player Development Centre. We . . .'

But the other boy wasn't listening any more. As soon as they could, Rob and TJ slipped away to join the rest of the boys in their room. The girls were in a separate dorm in a different part of the building. 'There was a kid on our table who plays for Aston Villa,' Jamie said. 'And another one who –'

'They were probably just making it up,' said Rafi. But he didn't seem too sure. 'And anyway,' he continued after a moment's thought, 'it's school teams we're playing against. Even if a team has one or two kids in it who play for an Academy, the rest of them are just like us, aren't they?'

'Maybe,' replied Jamie. 'But they made it sound like all of them were brilliant.'

The door opened and Mr Wood's head appeared. 'Bed,' he said. 'Lights out in five minutes, and don't stay awake all night talking. You've got a big day tomorrow.'

'As if we didn't know that already,' said TJ, as he climbed into his bunk.

CHAPTER 18

The next morning the boys sat together at breakfast. TJ didn't feel hungry, and he could see that no one else did either. They were looking around the room at the other teams, who all seemed to be having a great time.

'Hey,' said Miss Berry, arriving with the girls, 'why all the long faces? We're here. We're in the Regional Tournament. Cheer up!'

'Miss Berry's right,' said Mr Wood. 'And you have to eat. You've got a long day ahead of you. A very long day if you make it all the way to the final.'

'There's no chance of that,' said TJ. 'There are lots of kids here who play for Academies. They play for big clubs. None of them are nervous like we are.'

'Oh no?' said Mr Wood. 'I can tell you, TJ, that plenty of people make a lot of noise when they're feeling nervous. You lot are as good as any of them and I don't even have to see them play to know that. After all, you've been coached by me, and they haven't.'

There was a moment's silence, and then they all started to laugh. 'It's a game,' Mr Wood said, as he poured himself a bowl of cereal. 'You've done all the hard work, now you need to relax and play as if you were playing in the park. And you need to eat.'

TJ felt a whole lot better and he managed to eat three slices of toast. But when they reached the high school where the tournament was taking place, his nerves returned in force. The car park was full of coaches and minibuses and cars. People were milling about everywhere and TJ searched in vain for a sight of his family. He couldn't see anyone he knew. They went into the school and down a long, echoing corridor to a classroom that the boys were sharing with another team. Miss Berry took the girls away to their own changing room, and a few minutes later they all met up on the field.

Notices were pinned to boards on the edge of the field showing the groups for the first stage of the competition and the pitches where the games were to be played.

'That's us,' said Jamie. 'Pitch Five. We're playing Kingsmead School first, then Highfield, then Redhill. That doesn't sound too bad.'

'We're on first,' said Tulsi. 'We've only got twenty minutes and then we've got to play.'

'Good,' said Mr Wood. 'Let's go and warm

up. Oh, and Rob, I'd like you to be captain today.'

'But . . .'

'No arguments,' said Mr Wood with a smile. 'I know you'll do a good job.'

They found their pitch and saw that their supporters had arrived. TJ ran over to say hello to his family. There were dozens of familiar faces there: Mr Coggins in his ancient blazer, and the dinner ladies, and Mr Burrows and Mrs Logan. There were several other teachers too, and everyone's family. Although . . . TJ looked along the touchline and couldn't see Danny's mum anywhere. But then he saw more faces. Krissy Barton, Deng and Kelvin from Hillside School, and Leroy, the Wasps captain. 'What are you doing here?' he asked them.

'We came to support you, of course,' laughed Krissy. 'You're the District champions. You're representing all of us.'

'So you'd better win,' said Deng with his usual grin.

'TJ,' called Mr Wood. 'Get a move on!'

TJ joined in the warm-up. As they zigzagged in and out of a line of cones, he glanced over at the other team and was shocked to see the two boys from the night before. The curly-haired one and the boy called Bazza. He felt his stomach lurch, as he remembered that Bazza had scored goals against the Manchester United Academy. Jamie had seen them too. 'I hope you're feeling confident,' TJ said. 'I think you might have some saves to make.'

Kingsmead School won the toss, and the Parkview team took up their positions. TJ was starting up front with Ebony. Leila and Rob were in midfield, and Danny and Rodrigo at the back. Kingsmead kicked off and the ball was instantly played back to the curly-haired boy. 'Yes, Spike,' called a Kingsmead attacker – a tough-looking boy with bleached hair. Spike slammed a pass out to the Kingsmead left wing and TJ tracked back, trying to put pressure on the attacker. The attacker moved away down the wing, but TJ caught him easily. He was sure he could make the tackle, so he hooked his left foot around the ball. But the ball had gone, and his boot connected with the other player's shin.

The ref's whistle blew for a free kick, as the attacker massaged his leg. 'Sorry,' said TJ, offering his hand. 'You were too quick for me.'

The attacker got to his feet, ignoring TJ. 'You OK, Wes?' asked Spike, with a hard look at TJ. 'That was nasty, that was. Get in the area. I'll take this.'

TJ ran back, following Wes into the penalty area. The ball flew over his head and he heard Jamie shout, *'Keeper's!'*, as he rose above everyone to claim the ball. 'Get

forward,' he yelled, and he threw it out to Rob in midfield. Rob controlled it, then turned, looking for a pass, but all the Parkview players were closely marked. He gave it back to Danny, who picked out Leila on the right. Rob raced towards her, calling for the ball, and when it arrived he turned it neatly around his marker and into Ebony's feet on the edge of the centre circle. She took a touch. She yelled, 'To you, TJ!' But by then Spike had taken the ball away from her.

Spike's pass was genius. It was as good as anything Rob had ever done. He hit it with the outside of his left foot, curling the ball past Danny's outstretched foot and directly into Bazza's path. But Jamie was ready. He had seen the danger and moved out of his goal, and now he was facing the Kingsmead striker. He stayed on his feet as long as he could, but as Bazza lifted his foot to hit the shot Jamie dived to his right.

Somehow, Bazza had disguised the direction of his shot perfectly and sent Jamie the wrong way. Jamie stuck out a foot, but it was useless. The ball rolled into the net, and it was 1–0 to Kingsmead.

CHAPTER 19

'Come on, Parkview,' called Rob, as they kicked off again. 'We have to be quicker! We're going to have to fight for this!'

But although Parkview did their best they never managed to put any pressure on a ruthless Kingsmead side. Even when TJ managed to get a shot on target, late in the second half, the goalkeeper made a fine save, diving to his right. When the final whistle blew the Parkview players trooped off the pitch with their heads down. They had lost their first match 1–0.

'We're stepping up a level here,' Mr Wood

told them. 'So now you know what you're up against.'

'We've got no chance,' said Jamie.

Mr Wood looked at him sharply. 'Come on, Jamie,' he said. 'That's not like you.'

'Well, they did everything better than we did,' Jamie said glumly.

'That's not true,' replied Mr Wood. 'In fact, I thought it was a very good performance after you went a goal down. You fought for every ball and they simply couldn't get past you. Danny, that was outstanding. Now, we've got half an hour before our next match and I want you all to remember how we've practised keeping the ball. A good first touch and then make sure you don't give it away. There's some space over there where you can go and kick some balls around to keep warm. Try to relax. Oh, and Tulsi, you'll be starting this time.'

'I'm not sure I want to,' said Tulsi to TJ, as

they jogged over to the far side of the playing field. 'It looked really scary.'

'I'm sorry,' said Ebony. 'I gave the ball away and they scored.'

'Rubbish,' said Jamie. 'We were all slow. I should have saved that goal. He won't beat me so easily next time. No one will.'

Fifteen minutes later the team lined up for their second match against Highfield. 'You realize if we lose this then we're out,' said TJ to Tulsi, as they prepared to kick off.

'Let's not lose then,' said Tulsi grimly.

The whistle blew and she tapped the ball to TJ. He played it back to Rob and sprinted for the corner flag. It was a move they'd used lots of times, but this time the defender was ready, crowding TJ as he controlled the ball. He turned away from the defender, resisting his attempts to tackle.

'Yes, TJ!' called Tulsi, and he saw her

running towards him. He laid the ball into her path and raced past the defender, heading for the goal line. Tulsi played the return pass skilfully. He caught the ball just as it was about to run out of play and hooked it across the six-yard-box with his right foot. He saw Rob tearing into the area as fast as he could run, and for a second he was sure that Rob would score, but as Rob struck his shot a burly defender threw himself in front of the ball and it ricocheted out of play for a throw-in.

'That's much better, Parkview,' called Mr Wood, and for the first time TJ heard the sound of the dinner ladies chanting from the touchline. He ran across and took the throw quickly to Rob. Rob gave it back to him, and TJ saw his chance. He moved infield, teasing the defender who came to mark him, pretending he wanted to go outside, and then slipping past him on the inside. Rob

raced past TJ, bursting into the penalty area
again. A defender hesitated, then followed
Rob, and space opened up in front of TJ. He
took one more touch and then blasted a
curling left-foot shot into the top corner of
the goal.

TJ punched the air as the Parkview supporters celebrated. Then he heard Mr Wood's voice. 'Enough, TJ. Concentrate.'

He took a deep breath and jogged back. Seconds later he saw why Mr Wood had been so keen for the Parkview players to stay focused. Highfield attacked in force.

Every Parkview player had to get back and defend – even Tulsi. But Danny and Tommy seemed to be everywhere, and when they didn't manage to block a shot then Jamie saved it. At the end of the match TJ's goal was the difference between the two teams.

But they had all paid a price. 'I feel as if I've run miles,' gasped TJ.

'You have,' Rob told him. 'I expect you've run about—'

'Don't tell me,' said TJ. 'It'll only make me feel worse.'

'It's OK, TJ,' said Mr Wood. 'I'm going to

give you a rest in the first half of the next game. We'll see how Tulsi and Ebony do together. And Danny, you need a break as well. Tommy and Rodrigo can defend.'

'We've got to score some goals if we're going to go through,' said Rob. 'Redhill just beat Kingsmead two-nil over there. And they already beat Highfield three-nil.

Group stage of tournament after 2 matches

	Won	Drawn	Lost	F	A	Points
Redhill	2	0	0	5	0	6
Parkview	1	0	1	1	1	3
Kingsmead	1	0	1	1	2	3
Highfield	0	0	2	0	4	0

Redhill 3 - 0 Highfield
Parkview 0 - 1 Kingsmead
Parkview 1 - 0 Highfield
Final table Redhill 2 - 0 Kingsmead

	Won	Drawn	Lost	F	A	Points
Parkview	2	0	1	4	1	6
Redhill	2	0	1	5	3	6
Kingsmead	1	1	2	2	2	4
Highfield	0	1	2	1	5	1

It's lucky it was decided on goal difference and not on who scored the most goals
Parkview 3 - 0 Redhill
Kingsmead 1 - 1 Highfield

We have to beat them by three goals, and then hope Kingsmead don't beat Highfield by more than that.'

They all looked at each other. The idea of scoring three goals against a team that had just beaten Kingsmead seemed ridiculous. It was all as good as over. 'We should just enjoy ourselves,' said Jamie with a grin. 'What have we got to lose?'

'That's what I've been trying to tell you,' said Mr Wood. 'The ref is waiting.'

TJ felt strange, watching the game from the touchline, but he knew Mr Wood was right. He needed time to recover from all his running in the previous match. And as he watched, TJ could see that something had changed. The Parkview players suddenly seemed to have plenty of time on the ball, even though the Redhill players marked them closely. Rob was like a spider in the middle of a web, spraying deadly accurate passes around the pitch. They took Redhill by surprise, and a short distance along the touchline TJ overheard the Redhill coach turn to his assistant and say, 'I thought this lot were meant to be poor.'

'Oh no,' gasped the assistant. 'Look at that!'

Rob had chipped a pass over the heads of the Redhill defence and Ebony was onto it. She waited for the goalkeeper to dive at her feet and then lifted the ball neatly over his body and into the net. She didn't celebrate, but ran and picked the ball out and carried it back to the halfway line.

Suddenly, three goals looked possible after all.

CHAPTER 20

As half time approached the score was still 1–0 to Parkview, and they were still putting pressure on the Redhill defence. TJ was starting to wonder if Mr Wood would bring him on in this game at all. Tulsi had narrowly missed from the edge of the penalty area and Rob had seen a long-range effort saved brilliantly by the goalkeeper. It seemed as if it was only a matter of time before Parkview scored a second goal.

'What do you think?' TJ asked Danny, who was standing beside him on the touchline. When Danny didn't reply, he turned to look

at him. Danny was miles away, with a
worried frown on his face, not really
watching the game. 'What is it?' asked TJ.
He realized he hadn't had a chance to talk to
Danny since they'd been on the bus the day
before.

'It's my little sister,' Danny said, after a
pause. 'She was all hot and miserable and
Mum took her to the doctor. That's why I was
late for the bus yesterday. And I tried to call
home last night, and this morning, but no
one answered.'

'But . . . your mum must have said it was OK for you to come.'

Danny nodded.

'And if there was anything wrong they'd have let you know. We all had that letter with the number of the Youth Centre.'

'You're right,' Danny said, looking slightly more cheerful. 'Thanks, TJ. Hey look! Ebony's through!'

Rob had caught the Redhill defence out, playing Ebony in on goal with a single penetrating pass. But the last Redhill defender was fast. As Ebony hit her shot, he caught up with her and made a desperate attempt to tackle her. The ball hit his leg and ballooned into the air, flying over the goal-keeper's head and into the net. It was 2–0 to Parkview.

TJ found himself yelling at the top of his voice, but then he felt Danny grab his arm. 'Ebony's hurt,' he said.

Mr Wood ran onto the pitch. After a few moments he shook his head and lifted Ebony to her feet, then he helped her to limp painfully over to the touchline. 'Quickly, TJ,' Mr Wood called beckoning to him. 'Don't just stand there. You're going to have to come on right now.'

But before TJ could run onto the pitch the ref blew for half time. 'Is Ebony going to be all right?' asked TJ, as the Parkview players gathered around Mr Wood. 'It looked like it really hurt.'

'She turned her ankle as she shot,' Mr Wood said. 'She's OK, but she won't be playing any more football today.'

'How are Kingsmead doing against High-field?' asked Rob.

'You don't need to know,' said Mr Wood. 'If you win this game three–nil then you're through to the knockout phase. So you need to score one more goal, and stop them from scoring. That's your job. Don't waste time worrying about Kingsmead.'

As the second half began, Redhill made several dangerous attacks on the Parkview goal. Twice Tommy made crucial tackles, and once Rodrigo cleared off the line with Jamie hopelessly beaten. And in midfield Redhill had finally realized just how dangerous Rob could be. Every time he received the ball he found two players coming to mark him, blocking off the flow of passes to TJ and Tulsi.

The minutes ticked away and it began to look more and more likely that Redhill would score. When another shot from a Redhill attacker flashed past Jamie's post, Rob jogged over to Rafi. 'They're leaving you alone when they come to mark me,' he said. 'You have to get forward. Do one of those dribbles you always used to do and then get it out to TJ. I'll try and get in the area too. We have to score.'

Rafi grinned. 'We'll do it,' he said.

From the goal kick the ball came directly to Rafi's feet. He played it to Rob, just as he'd been doing all match, and the defender who'd been marking him instantly moved to cover Rob. Rob snapped a pass straight back to Rafi, who dribbled forward, flat out, into the Redhill half. TJ set off down the wing and Rafi found him with a pass down the line. As TJ ran he could see blue and black Parkview shirts streaming towards the penalty area, but Tulsi seemed to hesitate and TJ knew instinctively that she was doing what all good strikers do and making herself half a metre of space. As Rob and Rafi took three defenders with them into the area, TJ knew just where Tulsi would be. He pulled the ball back, wrong-footing every defender, and from fifteen metres out, Tulsi slammed it into the back of the net.

It was 3–0 to Parkview, and when the final whistle blew, three nerve-racking minutes later, Mr Wood was waiting for the victorious team with a huge smile on his face. 'You're in the quarterfinals,' he told them. 'Kingsmead only drew. Well done, all of you. I knew you'd do it. And by the way, Tulsi, you'll be pleased to know that our friends from the TV got some footage of you scoring.'

They all looked over and saw Maggie Burnside and a cameraman with the Parkview supporters. She gave them a little wave and a cheesy smile, but none of them waved back.

'OK,' said Mr Wood. 'Our quarterfinal is against St John's. They're one of the best teams here, and the main thing you need to know about them is that they're big and strong. They'll probably try to scare you with hard tackles. You'll need to move the ball quickly. Speed will give you an advantage. Take one of these drinks and an energy bar and be back here in half an hour.'

TJ jogged over to see his family. His dad was deep in conversation with Jamie's dad.

'Great win, TJ,' said his brother Joey. 'We all thought you were going out. Especially when Ebony got injured.'

TJ looked at his dad. 'What's up, Dad?' he said. 'You look like you're bursting to say something.'

'No,' said his dad, with another glance at Jamie's dad. 'I had a bit of good news, that's all. I'll tell you about it later.'

TJ laughed. His dad loved keeping secrets.

The Parkview supporters all moved over to the pitch where their next match was going to take place, and TJ got his first glimpse of the team from St John's. 'They're huge!' said his mum. 'They can't be under-elevens.'

'It's a big school,' said Mr Wood, who was

waiting on the pitch. 'And I reckon they just choose their biggest boys. Let's warm up, Parkview.'

It seemed to TJ as if time had speeded up.

Suddenly the warm-up was over, and St John's had kicked off. They played the ball forward and Rob intercepted the pass. He took one touch and a St John's player hit him with a crunching tackle. Rob crashed to the ground and St John's moved forward with the ball. TJ stared at the referee, who took a glance at Rob climbing to his feet and waved play on. 'Move, TJ!' yelled Mr Wood. 'Play to the whistle!'

TJ ran. This was going to be like no match they'd ever played before.

CHAPTER 21

A St John's forward thumped a shot at Jamie, but he got his body behind it and held on well. He raced to the edge of his area and threw the ball to TJ. TJ ran at a defender and then slipped it sideways to Rob, who moved it on to Leila before any of the St John's players could get near him.

'That's better, Parkview,' called Mr Wood, as Leila passed forward to Tulsi, who shielded the ball brilliantly before laying it off to TJ on the wing. TJ flicked the ball past the defender and nipped inside him, but the defender simply stood in his way and TJ felt as if he had run into a wall. He got to his feet dizzily, as he heard the ref's whistle. 'That was great, TJ,' Rob said in his ear, as he came forward to take the free kick. 'If we're as quick as that, they're bound to give away more fouls.'

'Yeah, and we'll all end up in hospital,' said TJ. He jogged into the penalty area. Rob's free kick floated towards the back post where Tulsi was waiting. She climbed into the air, but as she was about to head the ball TJ saw a defender nudge her in the back and it skidded off the top of her head and out for a goal kick.

'Hey!' said Danny, who had come forward for the set piece and seen what had happened. 'He shoved her, ref.'

Instantly the ref called Danny over. 'I'm the referee,' he said, showing Danny his whistle. 'No more arguments.'

'It's not right,' Danny muttered to TJ, as he ran back.

'It wasn't the ref's fault,' TJ said. Danny had been upset and worried about his sister before the game even started, and now it looked as if he might easily lose his temper, and that would be a disaster. 'He couldn't see. These St John's players are clever.'

'And dirty,' muttered Danny.

From the goal kick St John's launched another attack. Their midfielder turned past Rob, shoving him aside, and played the ball out to the wing. Danny saw where the pass was going and stepped forward to cut it out. He took a touch, then played it down the line to TJ, but as he passed the ball the St John's winger slid in to tackle him. The winger was too late, and he took Danny's feet from under him. Danny slammed into the ground. Instantly he was back on his feet, his face twisted with anger, facing up to the winger. Rob ran towards him. 'Danny, no!' he called.

TJ was certain that Danny was going to hit the St John's player and get himself sent off. But then Danny stopped. A voice was calling from the crowd. 'Danny! Hey, Danny!'

TJ looked. A tall, suntanned man was waving at Danny. He was holding Danny's sister, Rosie, in his other arm. Then he pointed to his side, and TJ saw Danny's mum with a double buggy beside her and two beaming twins sitting inside it.

Danny waved back. He had a huge smile on his face as he picked up the ball and waved the Parkview team forward. Tulsi collected his free kick on her chest and hit the ball back to Rob. Rob chipped it towards the corner flag and TJ hit the bouncing ball first time, back across the goal.

The defenders were too slow. Leila darted between two of them and slotted the ball into the net. It was 1–0 to Parkview and Leila just stood there, grinning. It was her first goal for Parkview, other than a penalty in the Cup semifinal. 'You need to think of a celebration that you can do every time you score,' Tulsi told her, thumping her on the back. Leila laughed. 'Great cross, TJ,' she said, as the Parkview supporters cheered from the touchline.

Suddenly the St John's players didn't seem scary any more. They just seemed slow. Tulsi began to make dangerous runs, pulling the defenders all over the pitch until they were breathing hard. Space began to open up for TJ and Rob and early in the second half they scored a classic breakaway goal, running the length of the pitch and exchanging passes before TJ fired low into the bottom corner for Parkview to take a 2–0 lead.

St John's were beaten and they knew it.

Tulsi and TJ each scored another goal and Parkview won the match 4–0. They were buzzing with confidence when they played their semifinal.Riverside School had no chance, as Parkview put three goals past them in the first half. TJ scored first with a header from a cross by Rafi. Then Rob put a curling free kick into the top corner before Tulsi scored, left-footed, from the edge of the area. The second half passed like a dream, as Parkview kept the ball with an exhibition of skill that had their supporters shouting '*Olé*' with every successful pass. And when the final whistle blew they were just one match away from being Regional Champions.

'This is it, then,' said Mr Wood, as they waited for the final to begin. TJ heard a shake in his voice and looked up. There was no doubt about it – Mr Wood was nervous. That wasn't surprising though. They were all feeling it now. A large crowd had gathered to watch the final and TJ had heard players from other teams saying that scouts from all the big clubs were here, on the lookout for talent.

'Excuse me, Mr Wood,' said Maggie Burnside, pushing between the Parkview players. 'I wonder if I could have a few words before the final. Jolly well done, all of you, by the way.'

'No, you can't,' said Mr Wood, putting a hand behind her back and ushering her firmly away. 'After the match, maybe.'

He turned back, and his face broke into a smile, as he saw a tall dark figure coming towards him. 'Marshall!' he said, giving his friend a hug. 'I can't believe you came.'

Marshall grinned at them all. 'How could I miss it?' he said. 'We played yesterday night, so we have a day off today. I drove up with Phil.'

TJ saw the coach from the Wanderers Academy standing behind Marshall. Phil winked at him, which TJ thought was strange. 'Marshall still thinks no one will recognize him,' Phil said. 'He's not exactly a master of disguise, is he?'

Marshall was wearing a black hoodie and a pair of dark glasses. 'I say, Marshall,' said Mr Burrows, coming up beside him. 'It's good of you to come. Good luck, everyone. You've done us proud even if you lose now.'

'But they're not going to lose,' said Mr Wood, smiling. 'Just as long as you all go away and let me get on with my team talk.'

'Well, do your best,' said Phil. 'Heath Road are a good side. They've got several Academy players in the team, but then so—'

'Phil!' said Mr Wood. 'Just go. Now then, you lot. This is what we're going to do . . .'

CHAPTER 22

Parkview began the final the same way they had finished the semifinal. As soon as the whistle blew, all of TJ's nerves evaporated and he could tell that it was the same for the others. They took control of the game right from the start and with five minutes gone the Heath Road players had hardly touched the ball. Both TJ and Tulsi had managed shots on goal, but the keeper had made unbelievable saves. 'We have to score soon,' Rob said, as Heath Road took yet another goal kick. 'They can't hold out for ever.'

Heath Road took a throw-in. Rafi was first to the ball, controlled it, and passed inside to Rob. Rob played the ball forward to Tulsi's feet and she turned it out to TJ on the wing.

'Come on,' said Rob to Rafi. 'This is it. Get in the area!'

They both sprinted forward. TJ took the ball to the goal line and pulled it back hard towards the edge of the penalty area where Rob volleyed it perfectly with his left foot. Rob was sure that he had scored. He started to turn away as his shot blasted towards the top corner of the goal, but then there was a loud crack as the ball hit the inside of the post. It rocketed across the goal, hit the other post and rebounded into the arms of the grateful goalkeeper.

The Parkview players were stunned and Heath Road were the first to react. The keeper threw the ball out to their unmarked winger, who flew down the touchline. Danny tried to close him down, but like all the other Parkview players he had been drawn out of position as they pressed forward, and he had no chance. The winger's cross came low and hard and the Heath Road captain, a tall boy, finished off the move by passing the ball elegantly into the corner of Jamie's goal.

For the rest of the first half, the game was evenly balanced. Parkview still had most of the possession, but they didn't dare to press forward in numbers again now that they had seen the power of Heath Road's counter-attack. 'You're doing well,' Mr Wood told them at half time. 'If you'd scored during that spell at the start it would have been a different game.'

'But we didn't,' said TJ.

'I've been thinking,' said Rob. 'What if we pull Tulsi back a little? TJ could play up front on his own and Tulsi can come from deep.

They might find it hard to pick her up. We have to try something different, don't we?'

Mr Wood smiled. 'You're still the Assistant Coach then, Rob? It's a very good idea. Let's try it. You're going to be like a ghost, Tulsi. They won't know where to find you.'

'She can do it too,' said TJ excitedly. 'In that game in training when Rob and the girls beat us. She lost me completely.'

'Off you go,' said Mr Wood. 'You have seven minutes to turn this around. You can do it.'

Heath Road pressed forward, trying to add to their lead, but Danny and Rodrigo kept them out, with help from the tireless Rafi who seemed to be everywhere. Then at last Rafi managed to squeeze the ball through to Rob. He saw Tulsi running towards him, drawing a defender out from the back, and he hit the ball over their heads into the space that Tulsi had left. Even as TJ was moving onto the pass, Tulsi had turned and sprinted diagonally across the defence. Nobody tracked her run, but TJ saw her out of the corner of his eye and switched the ball out to the left wing. He felt Rob slip past him, as he saw Tulsi collect the ball and hit a left-footed cross. Rob was in mid-air when he struck the volley. Somehow he kept the ball down and it flew into the net before the keeper could move. The scores were level at 1–1.

The Parkview supporters went wild, as Rob stood in front of them and pretended to write in his notebook, then held both arms in the air. TJ ran to Tulsi. 'Awesome!' he said, exchanging high-fives with her. 'Do you think we can do it again?'

'Why not?' grinned Tulsi. 'Hey, look, Marshall's blown his disguise!'

Marshall's hood had fallen back, as he jumped up and down and punched the air.

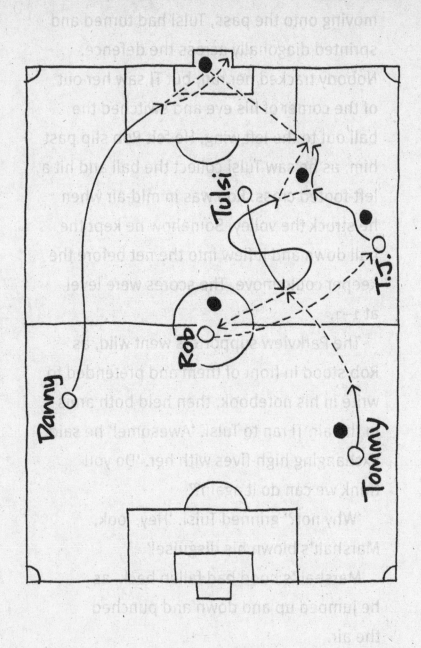

Maggie Burnside and her cameraman had rushed to film him and other spectators were pointing at him, but Marshall didn't seem to care.

'One more,' said Rob, clapping his hands. 'One more will win it.'

TJ looked at Rob. He couldn't believe he was the same quiet, slightly sulky boy he'd met on his first day at Parkview. Rob wasn't just the Assistant Coach, he realized. He was their leader.

Heath Road restarted the match and almost at once Tommy harried their winger into a mistake and came away with the ball. Once again, Tulsi came back, losing her defender and calling for the ball. This time she played a simple pass back to Rob and was off again, drifting into space. As TJ received Rob's pass wide on the right, he could see that the Heath View defenders had no idea what Tulsi was going to do next.

He cut infield, aiming for the edge of the penalty area, and a defender came out to meet him. Tulsi was free and she ran forward, offering herself for TJ's pass. He hit the ball hard to her feet. Tulsi swung round and played the ball back to TJ, who ran past the last defender and hit a low shot across the keeper towards the far post. The keeper dived and just got a hand to the ball, but there, ready to pounce, having raced the whole length of the pitch, was Danny. He blasted the ball into the net and raced away with his arms out like an aeroplane.

The score was 2–1 to Parkview. They were in the lead at last.

Rob and TJ chased after Danny and pulled him to the ground, as the Parkview supporters erupted. TJ looked over and saw Danny's dad with his arms raised high in the air, shouting louder than anyone.

But the match wasn't over. Mr Wood was holding up one finger. There was one minute left, and Heath Road threw everything at Parkview now. Their winger made a dazzling run that forced Danny to retreat. All Danny could do was force the winger out wide and try to prevent him from crossing the ball. But then, right by the corner flag the winger produced a piece of skill that fooled Danny completely. He hit a perfect cross towards the penalty spot and the Heath Road captain rose majestically to head the ball.

It looked a certain goal – but then Jamie took off. He'd had almost nothing to do in the second half, but he was ready. With the very tip of his fingers he touched the ball

onto the angle of post and crossbar. It flew
out to the edge of the penalty area and
Tommy belted it away, high into the air, as
the full-time whistle blew.

Parkview School were the champions!

Regional Tournament

Knockout Stage

Quarter-finals
Parkview 4 - 0 St John's

Semi-final
Parkview 3 - 0 Riverside

Final
Parkview 2 - 1 Heath Road

Parkview are
Regional Champions!!!

CHAPTER 23

'Great match,' said the Heath Road captain, shaking TJ's hand. 'Your striker played out of her skin in the second half. We couldn't get close to her.'

'Like a ghost,' grinned TJ. 'Yeah, she was good, wasn't she?'

Tulsi's gran was giving her an enormous hug. Danny was being lifted into the air by his dad. TJ's family surrounded him. 'Not bad,' said his dad. 'If you'd only tried that move I showed you once, then you'd probably have won by even more!'

'Right, Dad,' said TJ. 'You mean the move

that ends up with you flat on your back. No thanks!'

A man with a microphone was calling the teams together for the presentations. A table was set up near the side of the pitch with trophies and medals arranged on top. Maggie Burnside and her cameraman manoeuvred into position and several other photographers had gathered around. The semifinalists collected their medals first, followed by the Heath Road players and their coach. TJ and his friends applauded loudly. Heath Road had made the final into a match to remember – unlike the game against St John's. TJ could already feel the bruises spreading over his legs and side, as a result of that encounter.

'And now,' said the announcer, 'the Regional under-eleven Champions for this year are Parkview School. And as we have an unexpected special guest here today, I'm going to ask Marshall Jones to help our Chairman to present the trophy.'

'But who's going to collect it?' asked Jamie suddenly. 'We didn't decide.'

They all looked at each other, and then they all looked at Rob. None of them had any doubt. 'You're the captain,' TJ said to him.

'No,' said Rob. 'I can't.'

'Of course you can,' said Mr Wood. 'And they're right. It has to be you, Rob.'

All of the Parkview supporters cheered wildly, as the players walked forward one at a time to collect their medals. Miss Berry and Tulsi helped Ebony to walk between them. TJ felt as if he was dreaming as Marshall put the medal around his neck and shook his hand.

But it wasn't a dream. It was even *better*.

Then Rob was standing in front of the table and Marshall gave him his medal, and picked up the Regional Championship Cup.

'Before I present the trophy, I'd like to say a few words,' the Premier League player said, and the crowd hushed. 'Six months ago Parkview School didn't even have a football team,' he told them. 'Believe it or not, they didn't even have a pitch to play on. And now look at them! Regional Champions!'

There was loud applause.

'So,' said Marshall, when it had died down a little, 'it's my pleasure to present this cup to Parkview School.'

Rob walked forward. He had put his glasses on, and he looked a most unlikely captain, but Marshall handed him the cup and he lifted it high above his head, and TJ thought the cheering would never stop.

Finally the crowd began to break up and the Parkview players prepared to go and get changed. 'TJ,' said an unfamiliar voice, and TJ turned to see Danny's dad standing behind him, with little Rosie in his arms. 'I just wanted to thank you and your mum,' he said. 'Danny told me how you helped him.'

TJ felt his face growing hot. 'It's OK,' he said. 'We needed Danny in the team. You can see how good he is.'

'I can see how good you all are. I've been away working for six months and I come back and I find all this has happened. As if having two new babies in the house wasn't enough to get used to!'

'Are they OK?' asked TJ. 'Danny said one

of them was ill.'

'She's fine. They both are. And it looks like they and Danny have made a lot of new friends.'

A short distance away Danny was showing his baby sisters proudly to the rest of the team. 'Another few years and these two will be ready for our new Centre of Excellence for girls,' said Phil, who was looking on.

'You mean it?' said Tulsi. 'It's really going to happen?'

'Sure,' said Phil. 'And I'd like you to be a part of it, Tulsi. You were great today. You know how to lose a marker and you know how to bring other players into the game. If there was a Man of the Match award today, you would have won it.' He saw the look on Miss Berry's face. 'Sorry,' he said. 'I mean Player of the Match, don't I? And I'd like Ebony and Leila to come along for trials too.'

He looked over their heads, as they

hugged each other with excitement. 'Hey, Krissy Barton,' he called. 'Come here a minute. I wouldn't want you to miss out. It's not just going to be for Parkview players, this School of Excellence. You'll come along for a trial too, won't you?'

Krissy looked as if she was going to faint until Tulsi grabbed hold of her and started dancing around. 'I suppose you guys have told everyone your news?' said Phil to TJ.

TJ looked back at him blankly. 'What news?' he said.

'We didn't want to tell you before the tournament,' his dad said, smiling. He pulled an envelope from his pocket. Nearby, Jamie's dad pulled an identical envelope from his jeans. 'What is it?' demanded TJ.

'Can't you guess?'

TJ shook his head.

'It's from the Wanderers Academy,' Mr Wilson said. 'They want to talk to us, TJ –

me and your mum and you. They want to discuss whether you'd like to start a six-week trial. Jamie's got a letter too.'

'Actually,' said Rob's dad, who had been standing quietly in the middle of all the excitement, 'I got one of those letters as well. They want Rob to go along. I don't know much about it, this Academy. Is it a good thing?'

Everyone stared at him, and then they all began laughing and cheering. 'You bet it's a good thing,' said TJ, as the dinner ladies hurled their blue and white pom-poms high into the air and the Parkview supporters cheered on and on, and Rob's mouth fell open in astonishment. 'It's the best thing in the whole world!'

Who is Parkview's star striker?

Here are the goal scorers from this fabulous season, including all friendlies, league games, Cup games and Tournament matches.

Total goals scored: 54

T.J.	23 (incl. penalty)
Tulsi	11
Ebony	5 (incl. 1 deflection)
Rob	5 (incl. 1 penalty)
Raff	3 (incl. 1 penalty)
Danny	2 (incl. penalty)
Bela	2 (incl. 1 penalty)
Tommy	2
Rodrigo	1

And if you want to know how many goals were headers, chips or blasted into one of the top corners, you'll have to ask Rob!

Who is Parkview's star striker?

Here are the goal-scorers from this fabulous season, including all friendlies, league games, Cup games and Tournament matches.

Total goals scored: 54

T.J.	23 (inc. 1 penalty)
Tulsi	11
Ebony	5 (inc. 1 deflection)
Rob	5 (inc. 1 penalty)
Rafi	3 (inc. 1 penalty)
Danny	2 (inc. 1 penalty)
Leila	2 (inc. 1 penalty)
Tommy	2
Rodrigo	1

And if you want to know how many goals were headers, chips or blasted into one of the top corners, you'll have to ask Rob!

THEO WALCOTT

THEO WALCOTT was born on 16th March 1989 and grew up near Newbury. After joining the youth scheme at Southampton, he became the Saints' youngest ever player, before joining Arsenal in January 2006.

Following Theo's surprise selection in Sven-Göran Eriksson's World Cup squad, Theo set another record in making his England debut at the age of just 17 years and 75 days, and was named the BBC's Young Sports Personality of the Year in 2006.

Theo is now a star player for both Arsenal and England and in September 2008 became the youngest player to score a hat-trick for England.

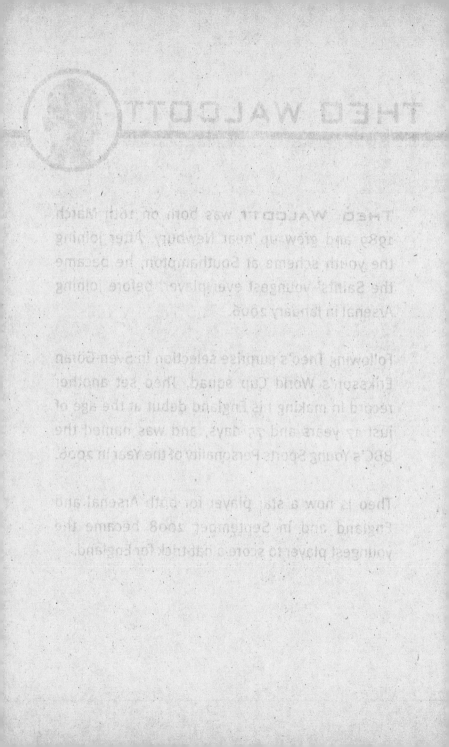

COLLECT THEM ALL!

T.J. AND THE HAT-TRICK

T.J. AND THE PENALTY

T.J. AND THE CUP RUN

ALL OUT NOW

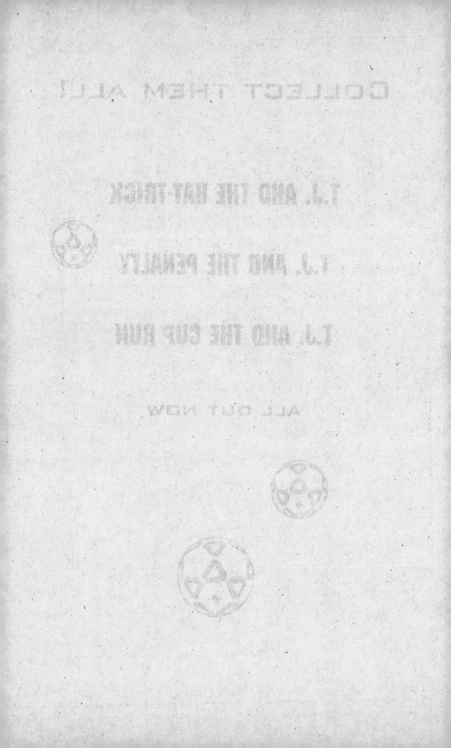